PRINCE OF FIRE

Warriors of the Fianna
Book Two

BY
SOPHIA NYE

ARE YOU SIGNED UP FOR DRAGONBLADE'S BLOG?

You'll get the latest news and information on exclusive giveaways, exclusive excerpts, coming releases, sales, free books, cover reveals and more.

Check out our complete list of authors, too!

No spam, no junk. That's a promise!

Sign Up Here

www.dragonbladepublishing.com

Dearest Reader;

Thank you for your support of a small press. At Dragonblade Publishing, we strive to bring you the highest quality Historical Romance from some of the best authors in the business. Without your support, there is no 'us', so we sincerely hope you adore these stories and find some new favorite authors along the way.

Happy Reading!

CEO, Dragonblade Publishing

Additional Dragonblade Books by Author Sophia Nye

Warriors of the Fianna Series
Song of the Fianna (Book 1)
Prince of Fire (Book 2)

The Warriors of the Fianna

Deep in the heart of the Kingdom of Munster, the legendary King Brian Boru has brought an ancient brotherhood back to life: The Fianna. Now entering his senescence, King Brian has all but achieved his dream of becoming High King of Éire, uniting the nine kingdoms to defend Éire's emerald shores from *Fin Gall* raiders. He will need the aid of the kingdom's best warriors to complete his vision and claim the seat of the High King.

But it is no simple task to become a warrior of the Fianna. Seven trials, the same seven used by the ancient Fianna, test the mettle of all who would claim such an honor.

Intelligence: Memorize the twelve books of poetry, so that you may be knowledgeable on the history, genealogy, and legends of your people.

Defense: With naught but staff and shield, defend yourself from nine men's spears while standing deep in a hole.

Speed: Outrun pursuers through a forest, without being injured. But take care! Not a branch may be broken to prove your skill.

Movement: Leap over a tree with a height to match your own, then crawl beneath a branch lower than your knee.

Recovery: Run through the forest with all speed until you step upon a thorn. Remove it, but don't slow down!

Bravery: Fight outnumbered without faltering.

Chivalry: Marry for love.

Truth in our hearts,
Strength in our arms,
Honesty in our speech.

DEDICATION

For all the women who have struggled with infertility.

You deserve every good thing that comes your way, and I hope they are many. You deserve happiness and joy and adventure. You deserve a book that doesn't validate true love with children. You are warriors. You are queens.

And, most importantly, you always have been and always will be enough.

CHAPTER ONE

Spring, AD 993
Kingdom of Laigin, Éire

NIAMH STOOD IN the courtyard at Nás, the stronghold of the kings of Laigin, utterly unable to stop laughing. Máire, her maid and dearest friend, fell into a fit of giggles along with her.

They had only been living in Nás for a few days, but the village had already charmed Niamh. Her father, a traveling merchant, had moved them into a larger town now that he could afford the expenses that came with it.

"What amuses you so?"

Niamh and Máire turned as one to face the young warrior who walked toward them. He was tall and broad, with a boyish charm and far too much confidence. His dark, wavy hair and smoldering chestnut eyes accentuated his strong jawline. And his cocky grin.

Instead of answering the lad, Niamh nodded toward the litter of kittens playing along the edge of the cobblestones. A dark grey one, the smallest of the bunch, attacked each of her siblings with vicious enthusiasm. The affronted, shocked looks the other small creatures gave the warrior kitten were simply more than Niamh and Máire could handle.

He watched the kittens for a moment, his brows knitted. "They are cute," he commented, clearly not as entertained by their antics. He leaned down to poke a finger at the grey kitten.

She bit him, hissing and jumping on his hand like she could

conquer anything.

He recoiled in surprise, frowning at the little beast disapprovingly.

Another sputtering laugh escaped Niamh. "She's fearless," she explained, taking pity on the confused warrior.

He grinned at her, his smile utterly disarming. "Aye, the smallest ones usually are, in my experience. She's going to be trouble."

"Or the best mouser," Niamh countered.

"Both, most likely."

"Don't let us keep you from your training," she told him, eyeing his sword, "I wouldn't want to get you into trouble."

He worried his bottom lip. The only sign that perhaps his confidence wasn't a bottomless well. "Actually," he said, running a hand through his dark hair, "I had hoped you might join me at training."

Niamh barely kept her mouth from falling open. How forward was he? To ask a woman he'd only just met to watch him train. Not that she wasn't interested, mind you, but he'd have to work harder than that for it.

"I'm afraid I'm quite terrible with a sword," she replied coyly. "I doubt sparring with me would improve your skills. I should hope not, anyway."

His smoldering eyes now sparkled with amusement. "I shall find another partner then," he conceded. "But I'd like for you to come, nonetheless. You can advise me at dinner tonight of any shortcomings you note in my form."

His boundless confidence was getting the better of her. Niamh had to admit she rather liked his bold manner. Not to mention his knee-melting smile and gorgeous eyes. He was certainly the most handsome lad who'd approached her, in addition to the most confident.

"And who says I'll be joining you for dinner?" she challenged.

"I do," he answered simply. As though they dined together every day. "If it pleases you, I can speak with your father first, but

I assure you it isn't necessary."

Niamh rolled her lips together. He was absolutely ridiculous. And she loved it.

"Very well," she conceded at last. "Máire and I are ready to be entertained."

He nodded to Máire in acknowledgement before leaning toward Niamh, his voice rough. "You won't be disappointed."

THE MYSTERIOUS WARRIOR made good on his word. He certainly did not disappoint. Though, as Niamh and Máire sat on their cloaks next to a group of noble ladies, also ready to be entertained, she realized that he hadn't given her his name. She considered asking one of the ladies beside her but paused when she looked at them more closely.

Every woman, no matter her age, wore elaborate plaits with golden beads and jewels woven throughout. Their silken gowns, brought to them from exotic kingdoms far from this small isle, shimmered in the morning sun. Sable and ermine wraps covered their delicate shoulders. Several women had not one, but two maids alongside them, and most sat on stools instead of the damp ground.

All of these women outranked her. Significantly.

Perhaps she'd have to wait and find out from the warrior himself.

The moment he entered the field, he turned and winked at Niamh. A few of the women beside her cast curious looks her way but didn't deign to speak to her. It didn't bother Niamh in the least. From that first look, she had eyes only for her mysterious warrior.

His lean, muscular body moved deftly against his opponents. Halfway through his first fight with a man so burly Niamh thought for certain her charming warrior couldn't best him, things took a turn. The burly man landed a solid blow on her warrior's chest, knocking him onto the ground. Niamh and Máire both gasped, along with most of the other ladies watching the spectacle. She would never forget the moment she realized that, perhaps, his boasting was not entirely in vain. Before the burly man could lift his sword, her warrior had spun, still on the ground, knocking the legs out from under his opponent. He pounced on him so quickly, sword against the man's throat, that everyone had shouted and applauded.

In the end, he won all but two matches. The first he lost because he was simply outmatched, fighting a seasoned warrior in his prime. The second he lost because he was making eyes at her and not paying attention. She had a good laugh at that, though she reluctantly admitted the lad was quickly winning her over with his charms.

He couldn't have been more obvious in his efforts to impress her. And still it was working.

As it neared midafternoon, the men wound down their practice. Gathering on the opposite side of the field from the ladies, they packed up their sparring equipment, stacking shields, swords, and spears neatly and efficiently. One or two men waved at the women who'd come to watch them. Then they all walked away in the direction of the river.

Except Niamh's warrior.

Bold as that grey kitten, ignoring the stares, he strode toward her across the field.

Niamh stood, waiting awkwardly as everyone watched their interaction. Her heart hammered in her chest.

When he reached her at last, he leaned down so that his lips were a breath away from her ears. "I'll see you in the hall for dinner."

It wasn't a question.

And even if it had been, the answer felt inevitable.

"I'D LIKE TO dine in the feasting hall tonight," Niamh announced as she emerged from her quarters into her family's small solar. Máire had helped her weave her hair into plaits, approximating the styles of the noble ladies as well as they could, even adding a single golden rose into one of them. She wore the nicest gown she owned, made of finely woven, deep blue linen.

Her father looked ready to argue, but her mother silenced him with a single glance.

"I assume we have an invitation to do so?" her mother asked, standing and motioning her own maid to help fix her hair.

Niamh swallowed, ignoring her father's horrified stare. She nodded.

"And who invited us?" he managed at last.

"I'd prefer not to say," Niamh hedged. "You'll meet him soon enough." She wasn't about to admit she didn't even know his name or lineage.

Her father's eyes widened, his frown deepening. "Him?"

"Oh, lord in heaven, Colban," her mother chided. "What else did you expect?"

"She could have made friends with a nobleman's daughter," her father argued sullenly.

Her mother just shook her head. "We don't want to keep him waiting," she told Niamh, gesturing to the door.

The moment her family entered the hall, her mystery warrior appeared, walking confidently toward her father. He extended an arm in greeting. "Master Colban," he began, shocking Niamh.

How did he know her father's name? They'd never even been introduced.

"Allow me to welcome you to my uncle's hall."

Niamh's breathing faltered. His *uncle's* hall? But that would mean…

"I am Dallan, son of Conn mac Murrough, nephew of King Morda, and Prince of Laigin. I hope you don't mind if I invite your daughter to dine with me?"

God's teeth, she'd been flirting with a *prince*? Her mother shot her an approving wink. Beside her, she heard Máire's sharp intake of breath.

Her father, rendered as speechless as Niamh, simply nodded and moved out of her way.

Dallan offered her his arm, guiding her toward the dais where the royal family sat. Everyone in the hall watched, an uneasy silence descending as she took a seat near the end of the king's table beside Dallan. Then the whispers began. Just as Niamh's nerves threatened to overwhelm her, Dallan turned to her.

"I'm sorry I didn't introduce myself earlier," he said quietly, keeping the conversation between just the two of them. "I hadn't realized I'd made such an oversight. Though, I have to admit, I do enjoy theatrics. I thought your father might faint for a moment."

Niamh giggled. "You should have seen him when I told him I wanted to come to the hall," she whispered back. "I thought his eyes would fall out of his head."

A scratching noise beneath the table caught Niamh's attention. She looked down, spotting an odd box between them on the ground. Before she could ask Dallan about it, he reached and pulled it into his lap.

"I hope you don't mind," he said gently, his voice like honey, "I took the liberty of getting you a gift."

Niamh opened her mouth to protest, but she shut it the moment he opened the box. The little grey kitten hissed wickedly at Dallan before leaping into Niamh's lap. Once again, the fierce creature brought a laugh to her lips.

"Your face lights up when you look at her," Dallan told her. "She'll need a name, though."

Niamh thought about it. Fierce and protective, utterly fearless. The wee thing was a born warrior. Many might see her as aggressive or even fearsome one day, but Niamh sensed a good heart, if a somewhat belligerent one.

"Morrígan," she decided aloud, testing the name. "Let's call her Morrígan."

"An apt choice," Dallan agreed, trying to pet Morrígan, only to be swatted at again.

As Niamh smiled for the hundredth time that day, she looked into Dallan's warm, brown eyes.

And she knew she was in trouble.

CHAPTER TWO

Spring, AD 994

H E WAS GOING to marry her.

Dallan had always believed that romance would never be a part of his life, that real love simply wasn't in his stars. He was the nephew and grandsire of kings. His marriage would be an act of strategy, and he had long ago come to terms with it. Or believed he had.

Then he met Niamh.

Year after year he'd teased and tormented the lads who pined after lasses, making spectacles of themselves only to have their hopes and dreams shattered. How foolish they'd seemed.

But one morn near midsummer, when he had only just celebrated his nineteenth nameday, Dallan became one of those lads he'd believed so foolish. On his way to the training field, he heard her laugh. The music of it sent a tickle down his back and compelled him to see who had made such a joyful, infectious sound.

The moment he saw her, he knew.

He would marry that woman.

And today, exactly one year after he began courting her, Dallan would ask for her hand in marriage. He'd already spoken with both their fathers and all that remained was her acceptance before a formal contract was drawn up.

The past year with Niamh had flown by in a flash of joy and discovery, a whirlwind of emotions he'd never thought possible, breaking down every barrier within him until all that remained was his truest self. And he meant to give that to her.

Dallan couldn't imagine life without Niamh. Indeed, it hardly seemed worth living. He waited for her in the meadow just outside Dún Ailinne, pacing anxiously. Normally he had nothing but confidence, but so much of his future hinged on this moment. It was difficult not to feel nervous.

In his closed hand, he grasped the ring he'd had made for her like a talisman.

She loved him; he knew she did. She'd said it many times and he'd seen the truth of it in her eyes. In the way she kissed him. In the way she'd melted into him as they lay in this very field many a night.

He was being ridiculous. Of course, she'd say 'yes.'

Dallan heard her soft footfalls and turned to watch her walk toward him in the fading daylight. Her hair fell about her shoulders, liquid gold turned to fire in the brilliant sunset. Her hips swayed as she moved, her grey eyes fixed on him.

"Niamh," he began, ignoring his absurd misgivings, "I have something for you."

She swallowed, worrying her bottom lip.

He took her hand in his, turning the palm up and placing the golden band in it. "It has sprigs of lavender etched along the outside," he explained. "I know how much you love them in the spring. The smell of them always makes me think of you."

Niamh took a deep, shaking breath. "Dallan, before you go on, there's something I must tell you."

A sinking feeling tugged at his chest, but Dallan brushed it off. Of course, she'd have questions, or things she felt merited discussion before making such a commitment. "Of course," he replied gently.

"My father spoke to me this afternoon," she began tentatively. Too tentatively.

Something was wrong.

"He told me that he approved of whatever direction I chose

to take my life." She paused, her cheeks flushing a pale rose. "I don't know if you are planning to propose marriage, or if I am getting ahead of myself, but I feel it is my duty to tell you this before we go any further."

His stomach tightened uncomfortably. "Tell me what?"

Niamh looked at her feet, blinking back what he desperately hoped were not tears. "I can't marry you," she whispered. "I'm afraid it's not possible."

Dallan felt as though he'd been hit by a spear, straight through his chest.

"Niamh," he managed, "if there's a problem, we can fix it together. I won't lose you without a fight."

"I'm sorry, Dallan. Really, I am."

"Is there another man?" he asked, unable to comprehend her sudden rejection of him. "I don't understand. Please," he choked, "please, just tell me why."

She simply shook her head.

"Niamh," he tried again, "just yesterday we spoke of our future together. Of the house we would build together. Of the children we'd have."

She started crying softly, sniffling and wiping tears from her cheeks. "I can't be your wife, Dallan. I'm so sorry." She turned her hand to give him the ring, but he stopped her.

"It was made for you," he told her, hoping she couldn't see how hurt he was, "you keep it."

He couldn't. Not after such a thorough breaking of his heart. He'd never be able to look at the ring again. At least if she kept it, it would see some use.

Maybe in the morn she'd see reason. She'd see the ring. And she'd come back to him.

Instead, the following morn her family packed up their belongings and left Nás far behind them.

First a week came and went. Then a month. Then a year. Then five more.

Still, he never heard from his golden-haired Niamh.

And still his heart refused to let her go.

In the end, he had been so much more foolish than those lads who pursued the glittering girls.

He had held her in his arms and still managed to lose her.

CHAPTER THREE

Autumn, AD 1000
Caiseal, Kingdom of Mumhain, Éire

DALLAN STRODE ACROSS the courtyard of the fortress at Caiseal in a stiff autumn rain, furious. Brian, king of Mumhain and his sworn liege-lord, had summoned Dallan to attend a visitor.

A visitor who should not have come, who could only have one of two reasons for coming to Caiseal and requesting an audience with Dallan.

Either his Uncle Morda planned treachery against Brian, or he wanted Dallan to swear his oath as second, heir to the throne of Laigin.

Dallan entered the solar ready to do battle if his uncle had come all this way to speak treachery in Brian's own home. Since he had joined the Fianna only a few weeks earlier, Dallan's loyalty had been split in two opposing directions. He didn't welcome the possibility of being forced to choose between them. It was a decision he hadn't expected to make for years.

Éire was divided into nine kingdoms, each one subdivided into smaller petty kingdoms. Dallan's uncle, Morda, reigned as the king of Laigin, one of the nine kingdoms. Mumhain, Brian's kingdom, was another. In the bloody battle over Dyflin, Morda and his cousin Sitric had lost to Brian, who had forced them to swear fealty to him as their overking. Though they kept their oaths, everyone knew it was but a temporary solution.

Technically, he could be sworn to Brian and also his uncle's second. Plenty of future kings swore oaths of loyalty and service in their youths. But he was no fool. Dallan knew that his family prepared to shake free from Brian's dominion at the earliest opportunity. Nay, he was no fool—and neither was Brian. Both knew that if Dallan became his second, it was only a matter of time before they were once again on opposite sides of a battle-field.

As he stepped into the large solar, Brian walked to meet him. Dallan had never been fond of the king, as his family had always been at odds with Brian's, but after spending some months in his service Dallan found himself gaining respect for the man.

"I'll be waiting for you in the hall," Brian told him before leaving Dallan alone with his uncle.

The moment the door closed behind the aged king, Morda walked to embrace Dallan, slapping him on the back and smiling wide.

"You've been gone far too long, lad. Your aunt will have my hide if you don't come visit soon."

The temptation of returning to the familiar pulled at his resolve. It would be a comfort to return to the place of his childhood, to the kingdom where his family had reigned for centuries, to the land of his birthright. But Dallan was not interested in comfort.

"I've only just sworn my oath to Brian," he replied. "And I cannot leave Eva or these men I've fought beside. I am needed here."

Morda nodded solemnly. Only a hair shorter than Dallan, his uncle was nearly a twin to both Dallan and his late father. "You've always been an honorable lad. And I understand your duty to Brian and your fellow Fianna. But Eva doesn't need you anymore. Is she not happily wed now?"

Dallan didn't like the ring of truth to his uncle's words. Only a sennight earlier, his sister, the entire reason he'd come into Brian's service in the first place, had been married to his best friend. Though Dallan couldn't imagine a better man to marry his little sister than Finn, a warrior who could play the harp as well as he could swing his sword, it irked him that he was no longer needed.

"Your family is calling you home, Dallan," his uncle continued. "I need you to stand beside me in the days to come, to learn to lead our kingdom. Eva doesn't need you here any longer, but I need you in Laigin, as my second."

Dallan took a step back, turning to face the crackling hearth fires. "I swore an oath, uncle. I cannot simply walk away."

"You swore an oath to your family long before the one you made to the Fianna. The time has come to uphold it. I'll give you a few days to decide, then I'll return for you."

Dallan nodded his understanding. Though grateful that Morda did not yet plot rebellion against Brian, his heart ached at the thought of choosing between his family and the Fianna. In the short time he'd spent with his fellow warriors, he formed bonds stronger than he'd ever expected.

He followed Morda from the solar, bidding him farewell in the courtyard before heading to the feasting hall to speak with Brian. Pushing open the heavy oak doors, Dallan found the massive hall empty, save for the wizened king in a chair before the central hearth.

Brian motioned for Dallan to sit across from him, smiling sadly as he did so. "I feared this very thing when you came here for your sister," the king began without preamble. "Tell me, what did your uncle want? Rebellion or you?"

"Me."

Brian leaned forward in his chair. "Family is everything. I've razed cities to the ground for the sake of my family, and I would do so again."

"I didn't agree to go with him." Dallan stopped himself from adding "yet" to the end of his statement.

"You've been loyal to me the entirety of our time together, to the point of defending my life from your kin. But you cannot swear fealty to both Morda and me. It would only work as long as the truce holds, and I know that will not be forever."

"What would you have me do? Forsake my family or betray you?"

"I would adopt you as my own son."

Dallan hadn't expected that. "To what end?"

"Loyalty. You would break all ties to Laigin, refuse the oath of the second, and join the house of Mumhain. You would, of course, inherit wealth but no title. You would be with your sister, remain with the Fianna, and gain renown as one of the best warriors in the nine kingdoms. And I would have no cause to question your loyalty again."

Dallan sat still as a stone, yet inside he reeled from the abundance of possibilities presented to him today. Return to his family and become a powerful king, keeping his people safe and living a life of service to his kin? Or forge a new family, bonded by the blood of combat, here with his brothers in arms and his sister? Though he knew his kin resented Brian's overlordship, Dallan had seen Brian's efforts to unite Éire and create peace for his people.

Was Dallan a king or a warrior? Did he belong to Mumhain or Laigin? Should he return home or stay with Eva?

"You and Morda have given me much to think on," he said at last. "I am grateful for your offer of kinship, and I will give it due consideration."

Brian stood. "I won't hold it against you if you choose your family, but you'll no longer be among the Fianna. Let me know when you decide."

Dallan watched Brian walk out of the hall. Tall and lean, without his grey hair it would be difficult to tell the king's true age. When Dallan first arrived at the Fianna trials, he had little respect for the king who had taken his sister captive. But, in spite of his best efforts, every interaction with the man only left Dallan liking him all the more.

No matter how long Morda waited to return for his answer, Dallan knew it wouldn't be long enough.

CHAPTER FOUR

Autumn, AD 1000
Thurles, Kingdom of Mumhain, Éire

NIAMH WATCHED WITH amusement as Morrígan crept up behind her mother, who sat mending a cloak, unaware that she was being hunted. When the mischievous cat finally jumped for the cloak's wiggling folds, her mother screeched, standing up to scold the beast.

Sitting on a stool nearby, Máire looked up from her embroidery, laughing at Morrígan's antics.

Her mother, fists on her hips and cloak still in her grasp, looked from Máire to Niamh. "It's a good thing that cat can hunt," she proclaimed, "else I'd be the one hunting her, the little terror."

"Morrígan has an excellent sense of character," Niamh replied evenly, turning back to her work table. She didn't have to look up from her mortar and pestle to know that her mother glared at her back.

Niamh's mother loved to complain about Morrígan, as had her father, but in truth everyone loved the house cat. She managed her little kingdom fastidiously, and even the neighbors noted how few mice or rats wandered the village streets.

After her father had abandoned them six years ago, Niamh and her mother had been able to use the money he'd left them to secure a small cottage. They even had enough to keep on Máire, who had become like a member of the family herself, but they had let all the other servants go. Between their remaining funds, their mending service, and Niamh's healing, they managed to get by comfortably enough.

"That smells wonderful," Máire commented once the room had calmed. "Is it cinnamon again?"

"Aye," Niamh answered, continuing to grind the sweet spice. "They finally had more in at the market."

Her mother, who had resumed mending the cloak, inhaled deeply. "Is Alva coming by again today?"

In answer, a knock sounded at the front door. Máire made to get up, but Niamh frowned at her and motioned for her to stay seated. There was no reason she couldn't answer the door for her own customer.

Opening the cottage door, she smiled warmly at Alva and invited her in. "I was just finishing up your infusion," Niamh told her. "How have things been going?"

Alva sat down in a chair at Niamh's work table with a defeated sigh. "Still nothing," she told her. "He'll be taking a second wife if I don't conceive soon."

"Oh, hush," her mother chided from the other side of the cozy room. "He'll do no such thing."

"He's said as much himself. I'm lucky he doesn't leave me entirely."

"Even if he takes another wife," Máire added, "you'll be his favorite. You're his first love."

"Now, ladies," Niamh interrupted, pouring boiling water over the ground cinnamon bark and adding orange peels along with it, "let's not get ahead of ourselves. Alva is going to conceive by the end of the year, or I'm going to resign as the wisewoman."

A raucous opposition sounded, startling poor Morrígan and sending her straight into Niamh's room.

"Niamh," Alva spoke over the other two, "I appreciate your efforts, truly. But I am not so foolish as to believe anything can be done outside an act of God."

"Then you'd best be praying to him," her mother muttered.

"He doesn't listen to us."

Niamh ignored the ache in her chest at her mother's words. "As long as Alva still bleeds, she can still conceive."

First her mother, then Máire, then Alva looked up at her. The pity on their faces made her want to scream. "Oh, saints, you lot. I'm perfectly happy without children."

It wasn't as though she had a husband she was trying to hold onto.

She'd made certain of that.

According to the laws of their people, a man could take more than one wife, if it pleased him. Most folk were happy with only each other, with one glaring exception.

Children.

The only men she knew who'd taken a second wife or who had left their women and remarried—her father among them—did so to ensure their family lines continued. Some women realized it was their husbands causing the trouble in conceiving and obtained divorces themselves. Really, folk could do whatever was necessary to have the children they desired.

Others didn't care whether they sired children or not. In fact, some of the poorer couples found it easier to get by with just the two of them to provide for. The folk who really needed heirs were the nobles, the lords and kings who had to throw themselves into battles to hold onto their power and protect their people. Aye, princes needed as many children as they could get.

Niamh glanced down at the gold band she wore on her middle finger, her chest tightening at the memories that came with it.

Niamh's bastard of a father had abandoned them after she refused Dallan's proposal six years ago. Apparently, he'd been considering leaving them before, but when he thought he might gain a connection to royalty through Niamh he had stuck around just long enough to watch her dreams crumble to dust.

Then, he'd left them. Because her mother had never conceived another child, and he had begun to worry over heirs and inheritance and lineage once his merchant empire had grown enough for those things to matter. Niamh knew it wasn't *really* her fault, as he'd planned to leave long before that, but she couldn't help but feel partly responsible for her mother's pain.

Niamh may be doomed to a life without love, but at least she wouldn't be forced to constantly face her own inadequacy with a disappointed husband. Her only regret was that she'd waited so long to leave him. If she hadn't gotten so carried away, she knew she wouldn't have hurt him as badly.

But that was her own burden to carry.

By now he probably had an entire brood of children, just as bold as their father. The thought that someone else had given them to him only deepened the ache in her heart.

But today was not about Niamh's mistakes. Today, she needed to help Alva shoulder her own burden. Unlike Niamh, Alva still had her monthly bleeding. Her body simply needed some coaxing to help her along. She picked up the pitcher and vials she had made up for Alva, setting them on the table between them.

"Apply this primrose oil to your wrists, temples, throat, and hips each morn and each night," she instructed, pointing to each container as she spoke. "I've made a tincture of milk thistle and raspberry leaves that you should take each day. Just pour a little out and drink it, but not too much. You can add honey if it helps the taste. Finally, this is an infusion of cinnamon bark and orange peel. Drink a cup every day. I'll have more when you run out."

Niamh may not be able to fix her own body, but she would do everything in her power to help other women fix theirs.

Alva thanked her profusely, heading home with an armful of hope.

Grabbing a willow basket from one of the hooks on the wall, Niamh donned her woolen cloak. "I'm going to pick some elderberries from the keep," she told her mother and Máire. "I'll be back this evening."

Just before she shut the door behind her, Morrígan shot out into the road, pouncing on an unsuspecting bug before turning to wait for Niamh. "Well, isn't that nice," she said to the cat as they walked up the hill to the keep. "I'd love some company."

Several hours later, Niamh laid in the grass beneath the grove of elderberry trees, staring at the cloudless blue sky. Morrígan had long since fallen asleep in the sunshine, her unladylike snores barely audible over the cheerful birdsong.

The elderberry harvest this year held great promise. A grove of twenty-odd trees sat right beside the keep, planted for this purpose many years earlier. Hundreds of berry clusters decorated the mantles of green leaves worn by each of the trees. She would be able to make enough syrup to last through the winter, and hopefully keep most of the folk from serious illness. Niamh had observed that if taken often during the cold season, elderberry syrup helped keep folk healthy. Once they developed a cough or a fever, however, the syrup alone wasn't enough to return them to health. She'd need many other herbs for that, and she'd only just begun stocking up for the long winter months.

Sitting up to return to her little cottage, an unwelcome chill sent shivers down Niamh's spine.

Something felt wrong.

Looking around, it took her several moments to finally realize what had changed.

The birds had stopped singing. Deafening silence surrounded her, interrupted occasionally by sounds from the keep nearby.

Niamh stood, gathering her basket of elderberries, and looking to the sky for signs of a storm. But there were none. It was as beautiful a day as you could dream.

Morrígan woke from her slumber, sitting up quickly, her ears perked and listening. Then she took off into the forest.

Niamh's skin tingled, as though her body sensed something her mind had yet to grasp. It wasn't unusual for Morrígan to spend days at a time exploring and hunting in the forest near Thurles, and her sudden disappearance wouldn't normally have given Niamh pause.

This time, however, Morrígan hadn't gone in search of something. She had fled. And when her warrior kitten went running,

Niamh knew trouble wasn't far behind.

She hadn't gone ten paces when the bells in the church started ringing. Looking up at the guard tower nearest her along the keep's palisade, Niamh watched as the men rushed toward the front gate, shouting frantically.

Then the first screams rose up the hillside from the village below. Followed by smoke.

Niamh's heart pounded. They were under attack. Dropping her basket of elderberries, she ran down the hill, making for her cottage.

And her family.

CHAPTER FIVE

Caiseal, Kingdom of Mumhain, Éire

DALLAN KNEW THE meeting would be called long before he stood in the corner of the king's solar. As he sparred with Finn, the only man he trusted with both his life and his sister, some of the other men spotted smoke on the horizon.

The eight men who had only just sworn their oaths as Fianna, an elite group of warriors in the service of King Brian Boru, turned aside from their training to investigate the smoke. In the field just outside the fortress at Caiseal, they stood in a line on the grassy hilltop.

Dallan. Finn. Diarmid. Conan. Cormac. Ardál. Illadan. Broccan. Out of fifty-three men who had undertaken the training to become part of the Fianna, they were the only ones who finished it. Some had simply failed. Many had died. And now the safeguarding of the kingdom fell squarely at their feet.

Dallan and Finn stopped to gaze at the white wisps climbing toward the clear blue sky.

"Where is that?" Ardál asked, taking several steps closer. "It's not Cill Chainnigh, is it?" He looked up at the sun to gauge the direction of the smoke, which now billowed ominously not a day's ride out.

"Nay," Illadan, the leader of the Fianna, shook his head. "'Tis Thurles."

"There's a rider," Cormac added, pointing to the man flying over the countryside toward Caiseal, pushing a destrier to its limits. "Brian will want us to go."

With all haste, the men headed for the solar, making it to the courtyard inside the keep before being waylaid by Dallan's sister.

Eva rushed toward Finn, her husband, the joy on her face bringing a smile to his own. Dallan had been furious when he first learned of his sister's love affair with his best friend. He had trusted Finn, and the betrayal had stung more than he cared to admit. But now he held them both in nothing but the highest regard. It had taken some time, mind you, but Finn and Eva had both proven trustworthy in the end.

Unlike other people in his life.

"You're back early," she commented, eyeing the other men who were even now piling into the solar. "Is something amiss?"

"It looks like Thurles is under attack," Finn told her, pulling her against his chest.

Dallan felt that he had intruded on a private moment, turning away to join the others in the solar instead of loitering in the courtyard. He also didn't care for the consideration of his own love life their romance had dredged up. He could certainly do without revisiting *that* ever again. All that mattered to Dallan was that his sister had found love, and that she could share her life with someone who loved her right back.

"Dallan," Eva called before he could disappear entirely. She pulled him aside, Finn hovering next to her, his arm about her waist. "You don't have to leave every time I hug my husband, you know," she teased. "I want to see you, too."

"I know," he replied. "I just thought you might appreciate some privacy."

"Are you still upset over the betrothal?" Finn asked, concern writ on his face. "What can we do to fix it?"

Dallan shook his head. "No, of course not. We cleared that up long ago," he grumbled. "You're both imagining things. I'm just fine. I was only trying to be polite."

"Are you still seeing that lady's maid? Ciara?" Eva asked, clearly unaware that there were far more important matters at hand.

"No," Dallan replied tersely. He'd never had the heart to tell her that the maid's recent boasts of bedding him were entirely fabricated. She'd been so happy thinking that he might have found someone that he never bothered to correct her. "And we need to get in there before Brian does. That rider will be here any minute."

"Dallan," his sister persisted, "you took a vow to marry for love. It's part of your oath, a responsibility you have now. You'll have to do it eventually."

She was right, of course. It was part of the oath each of them had taken to become one of the Fianna.

"I have every intention to," he informed her. "It won't be a problem, I simply decided Ciara wasn't that person. And it doesn't need to happen anytime soon."

His sister had the good sense not to comment further, but he didn't care at all for the look she gave him.

"What was that about?" Finn asked as they walked through the first set of doors leading to the solar, leaving Eva in the courtyard. "Do you mean to tell me there's a part of your life you haven't boasted of yet?"

Normally, Dallan would have shoved him into the wall of the corridor. Instead, he held his tongue and stayed his hand.

Finn stopped walking. "Gods, Dallan. Maybe we really should talk about this."

"It's something I don't much care to speak of, and I like thinking of it even less."

Finn furrowed his brow, staring thoughtfully at Dallan. "I'll try again when you're in your cups," he decided aloud.

That time Dallan did shove him.

They arrived in Brian's solar moments before Broccan, Illadan, and Brian returned from the barracks and the hall. Broccan had started assembling the army, and Illadan had gone to retrieve Brian and intercept the messenger.

Brian took a seat before the hearth, burning even during the day now that the weather had taken on the chill of autumn. Though he was but a shadow of the warrior he'd been in his youth, he still commanded any room he entered with ease.

"As you're aware, Thurles is under attack." Brian had never been one to mince words. "King Aodh of Ailech has come all this way south from Ulidia to wreak havoc on my allies. According to the rider I just received, King Cohal of Thurles is dead and one of his daughters has been captured. The village is burning, the keep has fallen.

"I am sending you to lead a contingent of men and retake the keep, securing it against further attacks. When Aodh has been dealt with, you'll need to retrieve the girl as well. Prepare to leave within the hour."

The men rode for Thurles straightaway, their mounts tearing up the dusty road that led from one keep to the next. 'Twas a short ride, not even two hours from start to finish. During the ride, they discussed strategies for retaking the keep, deciding they would need to scout out the location of Aodh's forces before making any final plans.

Upon arrival, 'twas clear the attack was all but complete. Aodh's men had secured the keep, the village still burning.

"He has men in the village, still," Broccan observed from their vantage point, lying flat on their bellies in the bushes outside the village. The army waited behind them out of sight.

At that statement, Dallan looked more closely at the movements of the men only to see the truth in Broccan's statement. A steady stream of villagers snuck past the marauding warriors and into the countryside. Far more, however, were trapped, pursued, captured, and wounded as the invaders went from cottage to cottage, pillaging and burning each one along the way.

"Why wouldn't they leave the villagers alive?" Finn asked under his breath. "If they mean to take the place of the lord, would they not need them?"

Dallan, nearest to Finn, turned to his friend. "It means Aodh isn't here for the lordship. He's here for hostages and heads."

"Aye," Diarmid, on Finn's other side, added. "Aodh is no fool. He knows he cannot hold a single fortress in the middle of enemy lands and so far from his own. He's not here to stay, just to destroy."

Dallan looked back to the scene before them, a grim one indeed. As he watched, a pair of men yanked a woman out of her cottage by her golden hair, grabbing her braid and pulling viciously as she screamed.

His stomach soured. The color of the woman's hair reminded him of Niamh, sending a shock of anger through him. Anger at Niamh. And anger at the bastard who would treat a woman so cruelly. Luckily, Niamh was safe somewhere far from here, he was certain, and unable to do any more damage than she had already. This poor woman, however, needed all the help she could get. When at last Illadan gave the signal, Dallan headed straight for the cottage and the woman with hair like spun gold.

CHAPTER SIX

NIAMH SPRINTED DOWN the hillside, herbs forgotten, stumbling over her own feet in her haste to get to her family. All she saw was fire. All she smelled was smoke. Destruction swirled about her in a blur of black, grey, red, and orange. Ash. Smoke. Blood. Fire.

"Líadan!" she shouted her mother's name as she neared their cottage. She still couldn't make out whether it was on fire, or simply surrounded by the smoke of nearby cottages. "Máire!"

She inhaled a deep breath of smoke, forcing her to stop and cough it out of her chest. Bent over double, she caught sight of the man coming up from behind her just in time to sprint the last stretch into her cottage. She slammed the door behind her, turning around and using her weight to hold it shut as the man tried to force it open.

Her mother and Máire shot up from where they'd been hiding on the ground behind her worktable, tucked in the far back corner of the room.

"Get that table over here!" Niamh shouted, gesturing at them to hurry. "We must bar the door and get out the back! They're torching all the cottages!"

The two women worked to carry the heavy table over to Niamh.

The door behind her flung open a hand-span before it thumped shut again.

She couldn't hold it much longer.

They tipped the table on its side.

The door thumped again.

A sinking feeling took hold in the pit of Niamh's stomach. She realized now that the moment she moved to let them pin the door with the table, it would instead fly wide open.

"Run out the back," she told them, her voice trembling. "Go."

"God will break his own legs before I leave my only daughter to die," her mother grumbled, moving to stand beside her and help hold the door closed.

Máire followed right behind her, glaring pointedly at Niamh for her attempted bravery. "We'll never leave you behind," she whispered, grimacing as something remarkably heavy hit the door.

Twice more, the door shook behind them.

The third time, it opened completely. Two men barreled through the doorway, dropping torches and setting the cottage ablaze as they entered.

Máire screamed. Her mother fell forward, landing against the table.

Niamh's heart raced, her head feeling too light.

The first man went after Máire, dragging her toward the back of the cottage. The second grabbed Niamh's braid, pain shooting through her head as he yanked her out of the threshold.

She screamed, unable to keep herself quiet as he pulled her outside.

Away from Máire. Away from her mother.

The angriest yell she'd ever heard sounded from her feet. Though her vision blurred in pain, Niamh still could see Morrígan, preparing for attack. Just as she did with the mice. She must have followed Niamh from the keep.

Lord bless that little warrior. She really thought she could do it, too. Niamh saw it on her face.

The cat spat and hissed, jumping at the brute's feet and legs. He swore, kicking Morrígan away, far harder than the wee thing needed. She flew backward, hitting the pile of firewood stacked beside the cottage and crumpling to the ground.

Niamh shrieked, doing her best imitation of the cat and tearing viciously at the man holding her, trying not to think on how Morrígan fared after that blow. She knew she could do little to free herself, but hopefully she could at least make things more difficult for him.

She reached for her captor, spinning toward him.

And missing wildly.

Now that she faced away from her cottage, however, she could see the village on fire before her.

And running through the burning wreckage, sword in hand, was a man she never thought she'd see again. Her heart faltered. Her mind spun.

How could it be?

And yet there he was, the man who'd filled her dreams since the day they'd met seven years ago.

He charged toward them, a violent promise on his beautiful face.

DALLAN HAD NEVER been angrier in his life, and that included when he had discovered his best friend was bedding his sister.

The chances that he would see Niamh again, and at such a crucial moment, were beyond reckoning. Yet here he was, rushing up to save her as though they'd never parted paths.

The bastard never saw him coming. He was too focused on Niamh, something Dallan understood all too well.

"Down!" he shouted to Niamh, who obediently fell to the ground, shrieking as her plait pulled taut in the man's grip.

He fell in a crumpled heap beside Niamh as Dallan's sword slid back out of him, covered in blood.

For several breaths, neither moved. Niamh looked just as

shocked by his appearance as he had been by hers. As the urge to hug her came over him, Dallan forced them both to action.

"You need to get out of here," he growled, offering her his hand and pulling her up from the ground.

"Máire!" she shouted, as though just recalling her maid. "The other man, he took her inside." Without waiting for Dallan, she spun around and charged back inside the house.

"Woman!" Dallan shouted in frustration, reaching for her and missing as he attempted to keep her from getting herself killed.

She ignored him. Unsurprisingly.

He rushed to get to the man before her, entering the small cottage and following the screams to a back room. It seemed he'd arrived just in time.

Again.

He shouted to distract the man who was clearly attempting to remove Máire's clothing. The maid proved feisty, though, and Dallan noted the multitude of scratches on the man's face and arms.

The man turned toward Dallan, wielding a short sword, a dagger, and one hell of a grumpy face. He lunged. Dallan parried, then charged him, pinning him against the wall so that Niamh and Máire could get out of the room. In a few quick exchanges of their blades, Dallan had easily bested the man, as would be expected of one of the Fianna.

He didn't tarry even a moment, returning quickly to the main room of the cottage, which was filling with smoke at an alarming rate.

Niamh and Máire kneeled beside an old woman, whom he recognized as Niamh's mother, Líadan. She'd been wounded, a trickle of blood dripping down her forehead and onto her cheek. All three women noticed his presence at once, turning in unison to stare at him with varying degrees of shock and gratitude.

For the briefest time, Dallan forgot how to breathe. All the memories of his time with Niamh flooded his mind.

Laughing with her over her ridiculous kitten.

Her golden hair falling into his face as she lay over him in the summer meadows.

Dancing with her around the Samhain bonfire, their hands locked, their eyes fixed on one another.

The look on her face when she turned away from him.

The pain that followed when she broke his heart.

Finally regaining control of himself, he pinned her with a look that told her precisely how he felt about seeing her again.

Furious.

She stood, either oblivious or impervious to his death glare, and took a step toward him.

"No," he growled, his voice low and dangerous. "You need to leave. Now."

"He's right," Máire agreed, still crouching beside Líadan. "They're still burning cottages."

Niamh stopped then, and Dallan prayed to the lord almighty she would just leave him be. He couldn't let her near him again.

"Thank you," she whispered, turning to help her mother stand.

Dallan moved around them, walking out the door first to ensure the way to the forest was clear of Aodh's men. "Hurry," he called, moving to circle the cottage as the women helped Líadan hobble out.

Niamh flew out of the burning cottage, rushing over to the wood pile. Dallan watched her in confusion as she picked up something, cradling it like a babe. She turned back to face him, tears in her eyes, leaning her ear to a ball of dark grey fluff.

Dallan closed his eyes with a sigh. Morrígan.

Swallowing his anger, he reached for the fluffball, pressing his hands along her sides to try to find signs of life. The fact that the beast wasn't attacking him was cause for concern indeed.

"She tried to save me," Niamh told him with a sniffle, tears now flooding her cheeks. "She charged right at him."

"She's as fierce as they come," he replied quietly, himself beginning to worry.

The golden-haired beauty was falling apart, shaking more and more as she held Morrígan. For the first time since he arrived at her doorstep, Dallan captured her eyes and didn't glare at her.

"She lives," he told her, "I can feel her breath."

His words only caused more tears to flow as Niamh snuggled the cat to her.

"You need to get your family out of here," he reminded her, looking about again to ensure they were still safe. "Aodh's army isn't far, and he may return. Head south toward Caiseal."

She nodded numbly, cradling the cat in one arm and offering the other to her mother, who had appeared beside them without Dallan's realizing it.

They moved slowly, Líadan clearly in a good deal of pain with her injuries. Dallan stayed outside their cottage, monitoring their progress until they reached the cover of the trees.

Just before ducking into the forest, Niamh turned to look at him. She started waving, motioning, but he couldn't understand what she tried to tell him.

He squinted.

She shouted.

Then the world went dark.

CHAPTER SEVEN

"**G**ODS, MAN! WHAT'S the matter with you?" Finn shouted from above him.

Dallan's left temple throbbed and his shoulder burned like he'd been branded. A hand appeared in front of his face. Shaking off his confusion, Dallan took it, moving too quickly to his feet. He swayed as he struggled to regain his balance.

"What happened?" Finn asked, furious. "I leave you alone for mere moments and by the time I find you, you've nearly gotten yourself killed! You're lucky Illadan didn't see such a lapse."

Dallan couldn't agree with him more. "I was acting the fool," he muttered. "I'm fine now."

Finn looked pointedly at his shoulder, frowning. "You'll need a healer with a wound such as that. They've sent a search party to find the village wisewoman. Many wounded wait for her up at the keep. Let's get you up there to join them." Finn took off Dallan's cloak and tied it about his shoulder quickly and tightly, staunching the flow of blood that Dallan had hardly noticed.

Narrowing his eyes, Finn regarded him. "Are you alright?" he asked, his voice filled with concern. "You don't seem yourself."

Dallan swallowed. He was many things at the moment; 'alright' was not among them. "I'm fine," he lied, walking away from Niamh's burning cottage. "Let's get to the keep."

As they passed through the smoldering village, Dallan turned several times to make certain Niamh hadn't reappeared. Worse than seeing her again, worse than reopening that deep wound, was something that terrified Dallan to his very soul.

Even after all that had happened between them, the moment she disappeared Dallan started missing her all over again.

Together the two warriors walked through the remains of the village toward the keep. This was Dallan's first opportunity to really take in the destruction in the wake of the bloody battle. Aodh had attacked the villagers, not just the lord in his keep. Which meant he hadn't come for the keep.

He'd come for blood.

"We routed them, then?" he asked Finn, not seeing other warriors anywhere.

Finn nodded but furrowed his brow. "'Tis more complicated than just that, I'm afraid. We've retaken the keep and driven Aodh's army back north, but Broccan and Illadan worry that his allies will come in a second wave. Or that he'll divide his forces, circle around, and head straight for Caiseal."

"Who's watching them?" Dallan knew Illadan wouldn't stop following Aodh until he was certain of their full retreat.

"Conan and Cormac went after them with five of Brian's men. The rest of the Fianna are meeting in the keep to discuss our next steps."

Dallan looked askance at Finn. "Not Conan and Diarmid?" he asked. The brothers were hardly ever apart from one another. Though Cormac was also their brother, he kept far more to himself.

Finn grinned at that question. "Ah, yes. The, uh, lady of the house is a bit stubborn, but she's quite taken by our Diarmid's undeniable charm. He's the only one she'll listen to so far, so Illadan kept him around."

Dallan chuckled. Of course. Nothing about that surprised him in the least.

They climbed the hill up to the keep, Dallan's shoulder bothering him more the further they went. He bit back a grunt of pain as they neared the top of the hill. His wound needed treatment, though it was far from fatal. He could wait until meeting with the men to see the healer.

The keep was smaller than Caiseal, yet large enough to hold a good many guests in the great hall. The solar couldn't accommodate all who needed to attend the meeting. The hall was rectangular, having been rebuilt in the newer style recently, but still had the hearth in the center of the room, its hot flames licking the iron grate that surrounded them. Wooden rafters formed a vault toward the center of the room, and the traditional alcoves lined the farthest walls.

In the center of the room, standing around the crackling fire, the Fianna stood, waiting. A woman of middling years, her dark hair woven into elaborate plaits atop her head, sat upon the dais in the queen's chair. Undoubtedly, this was King Cohal's wife, Queen Brona. Her back was straight as an arrow, her hands folded in her lap, as she gazed down her nose at the men before her.

He looked at Finn, who rolled his eyes. His brother-in-law was a good man. The best, in fact, else Dallan would never have agreed to his sister's marriage. But Finn had no tolerance for entitled nobles, even those he was meant to save.

Dallan, on the other hand, understood Brona all too well. Her husband had been killed, she'd lost her keep and a daughter to an invading army, and King Brian's men had won it back. No doubt she worried over her place after such a debacle. Setting a strong example from the outset was in her best interest.

"You need a healer," Diarmid remarked, looking at Dallan's shoulder with furrowed brows as they walked to stand near him. "Illadan!" he called, not waiting for Dallan's response. "Has she been found yet? The healer?"

Illadan strode over to them, himself inspecting the wound. "She hasn't," he mumbled, leaning closer to get a better look.

"Oh, for the love of Christ," Dallan muttered in frustration. "You lot act like you've never seen a stab wound before."

Illadan narrowed his eyes at Dallan. "I haven't on one of the Fianna. You were being careless."

"I was." Dallan wouldn't even attempt to deny it. Everyone knew it was the only way he'd have been injured in such a minor skirmish. "It won't happen again."

"No," Illadan replied coolly. "It won't. You'll be staying here to guard the keep as penance for your poor judgment."

Dallan didn't argue. He'd been trained better than that, though he tightened his fists at his own stupidity. Niamh had always had a way of getting to him. It seemed time hadn't changed that one bit.

"Now that we're all here, let's get this over with. We have much to do, and no time to waste," Illadan declared, stepping to the center of the group, next to the flames. "Conan and Cormac are tracking Aodh's men to ensure they stay the course north. We don't trust him to make a full retreat, and we will pursue him back to his own territory.

"Broccan, Conan, Finn, Ardál, and I will lead two-thirds of Brian's hosting northward in pursuit of Aodh and to rescue Lady Cara. Cormac, Diarmid, and Dallan will remain here to ensure one of Aodh's allies doesn't follow with a second attack on Thurles. Brona will manage the holding, excepting the fortifications and guardsmen. Is everyone in agreement?"

"How will you recover my daughter without endangering her further?" Brona asked, her voice wavering.

Broccan, the leader of Brian's army and one of the three leaders of the Fianna, turned to face her fully. "It depends entirely on the manner in which she is being held when we come upon her. But you have my word we will do nothing to endanger her further. She will be returned to you safely, should she yet live."

Brona swallowed hard at that statement but kept her composure. A commendable feat for anyone after all she'd been through this day.

Illadan looked to the men he'd named to pursue Aodh, instructing them to ready to leave before the next bell. Then he looked at Dallan. "Get yourself to the infirmary. Finn, help him before you go."

"I'm perfectly able to get myself to the infirmary without a nursemaid," Dallan muttered.

"Aye," Illadan agreed, "but I've no guarantee you'll stay there and wait for the healer to be found. You're more stubborn than I, and that's a notable accomplishment."

"He's not wrong," Finn added unhelpfully, shoving his good shoulder toward the exit. "It's near the chapel."

They walked across a fine stone courtyard, passing the stables and the chapel before reaching a building much like the hall. Inside, two dozen men and women lay in varying states of injury, from minor flesh wounds to missing limbs. The rusty smell of blood and the noxious scent of festering flesh filled Dallan's lungs. Fighting back the urge to gag, he quickly backed out of the room.

"You have to stay and see the healer," Finn reminded him.

"I'll wait out here," he declared, sliding down the side of the building until he sat on a pile of wood.

Finn frowned but didn't argue with him. "I'm coming back here to check on you before I go, and your sorry arse had better be here or you'll need more than a healer."

Dallan chuckled at Finn's idle threat. "What? I'll need a priest?"

"Don't make me do it. It'll upset Eva."

"Fine, fine," Dallan waved him away. "I swear I'll behave."

Finn turned, leaving Dallan alone with his thoughts. Thoughts he'd been trying not to acknowledge, that brought back feelings and memories he'd prefer to leave in the past.

But it seemed his past had finally caught up with him. As though the very thought summoned her, Niamh appeared in the courtyard, walking straight toward him. But she hadn't noticed him, not yet. She carried a satchel over her shoulder and a pile of linens in one arm. Her eyes held a faraway look he didn't care to wonder about. She stopped abruptly when she finally realized he sat in front of the building.

"What are you doing here?" he asked, unable to hide his frustration at seeing her again. "I know you aren't here to check on me, since that would require you to *feel* something toward me."

A flash of hurt crossed her face, and he nearly regretted his words. Nearly. If she hadn't ripped his heart out a few years back, he might have some pity for her. At present he couldn't muster anything other than anger.

Shifting the pile of linens, she looked at his shoulder. Not meeting his gaze. "I'm the healer."

Dallan blew out a frustrated breath. "Of course you are."

CHAPTER EIGHT

S HE DESERVED THAT. And more. Niamh knew how deeply she'd hurt him. Part of her wanted to reach out to him, to find a way to make it up to him. But she knew exactly where that would lead, and it would only hurt them both.

If he knew her secret, he might actually forgive her. Which was why she hadn't told it to him that night so long ago, in another life filled with happiness and hope. A life with possibilities. The last thing she wanted to give either of them was hope. She'd learned at a young age that hope was a dream that never came true.

So, instead of reacting to his venom, she let it seep into her. It was the least she could do, after all.

Swallowing the pain his words caused, she looked at the ground, not ready to face his anger. "I'll need to tend to the most injured first," she told him quietly. "I'll be out shortly to see to your shoulder."

His silence followed her into the putrid infirmary.

The priests had all been killed. To what end, Niamh didn't try to determine. Had they lived, many of these wounded would have already begun healing before her arrival. She'd often worked with Father Tomás and Father Sean, both skilled healers in their own rights. Their loss was beyond words.

Now all the injured fell to her. Swallowing the bile rising in her throat, Niamh wandered through the room purposefully, taking mental note of the extent of each person's injuries. Tadhg, who'd taken a blow to the thigh, was most in need of her attention. Rolling up her sleeves and calling for men to hold him down, she set to her most unpleasant task.

Time held still as she moved from patient to patient. By the time she'd made her rounds and Dallan's wound was the next to tend, it seemed as though she'd only just spoken with him. Before she ventured back out, Niamh stopped at a small pile of blankets on her worktable, checking to be sure Morrígan was still breathing. She'd managed to patch up the wee thing, who'd been sleeping peacefully ever since—a sure sign something was wrong. At the gentle brush of Niamh's fingers on her soft fur, Morrígan half-opened an eye, purring contentedly before returning to her healing slumber.

Stepping out into the fading light of late afternoon, she'd half-expected him to be gone, unwilling to face her long enough to be treated. Disappointment and excitement both hit her full-force when she spotted him exactly where she'd left him.

He stared at her, still unnervingly silent. His chestnut eyes threatened the shred of calm that remained after seeing so many grotesque injuries at once.

She knelt before him, setting down the bowl of water, bandages, and healing herbs she'd brought to treat him. "You'll need to remove your *léine*," she whispered, waiting for his barb.

Instead he complied without complaint.

When she looked up at him, he gazed heavenward and heaved a sigh, clearly seeing her confusion.

"I'm not a beast," he grumbled. "I heard what you went through in there. I'll be nice. For now."

Niamh swallowed, worrying her bottom lip. It was easier when he was angry. If he kept treating her kindly, it would only get harder to stay away from him.

Not trusting herself to speak, she simply worked. Washing his wound, packing it, and wrapping it with clean linen. It took only minutes. As she picked up her supplies, she realized that he was staring at her hand.

He'd spied the ring she wore. The one he'd given her the night he asked for her hand in marriage.

Cursing her carelessness, she used that hand to hold the linens, hiding the ring from sight. "I'll need to check on your wound in the morn and repack it," she told him quickly, lest he get some grand idea to comment on the ring and wonder aloud at why she wore it.

"Shall I come here, then?" he asked coolly.

"Aye," she muttered, hurrying back to the safety of the infirmary. Two patients yet waited for her whose injuries were slight.

She'd never been more grateful to have injured folk to tend. Not stopping to think on Dallan at all, Niamh headed off to her next patient.

SHE WAS WEARING the ring.

Why was she wearing the ring? Was she toying with him? Had she put it on deliberately to attempt to win his affections back? To what end?

Nay, she was cruel indeed but not malevolent. And she hadn't known he'd be there, had she? Which meant that she'd been wearing it all day.

But why?

She hadn't wanted to marry him, yet now she wore his ring. Perhaps she was trying to scare off an unwanted suitor. Aye, that was it. She probably had dozens of men throwing themselves at her feet.

It mattered not. He wasn't going to succumb to her charms again. He had no desire to let her in only to have his heart broken once more. The anger he felt served as a convenient shield for any other feelings, and it was no farce. That she could leave him, when they'd been nearly betrothed, without any reason for it, filled him with untampered fury.

He'd gone easy on her after hearing the screams of the folk who'd needed serious treatments. Unsettling didn't quite capture the afternoon he'd had. Harrowing, perhaps. Either way, she'd not needed his spiteful comments then, so he'd kept his silence.

"You look worse, not better," Finn called, alerting Dallan to his approach. "I'd hoped seeing the healer would improve your condition."

"I need a different healer," he replied, hoping this would keep Niamh far from him. "She's no good."

Finn folded his arms across his chest, raising an eyebrow. "Brona says she's the best healer they've had in twenty years or more. Even the priests deferred to her knowledge."

Dallan wouldn't give up so easily. His sanity depended upon it. "Is there no one else who could change the bandages?"

Finn shook his head. "All the other healers were priests. None of them were spared."

Dallan swore under his breath.

Finn sat down next to him. "I have just long enough before I leave for you to tell me what in the world has you so unbalanced."

Peeking around the corner into the infirmary to be sure she was out of earshot, Dallan reluctantly turned to his friend. "Niamh," he whispered.

"The healer?"

Dallan nodded. "Do you recall earlier today, Eva mentioned her concern over my ability to fulfill my oath?"

"Ah, yes," Finn jested, "Just before you became unreasonably irritable, you mean?"

"Yes," Dallan ground out. "The healer—" he wasn't even certain where to begin. He'd never explained his relationship with Niamh to anyone, not even his sister. "I loved her. Deeply."

"And it didn't go well."

"Well, we aren't married, are we?" he shot back. "I'm sorry," he added. "I just cannot believe how unlucky I am to see her again. It's been so long."

"What happened?"

Dallan took a deep breath, not letting himself feel the memory, telling the story as though it didn't matter a whit to him.

When he'd finished, Finn shook his head. "You're looking at it all wrong," he whispered. "This is your chance. This is the opportunity you've always wanted, to get your answers. Play nice with her and get her to finally tell you why she left. Then you won't have to spend the rest of your days wondering. You'll be able to let her go."

He hadn't considered that.

Finn stood, taking his leave to head out with the search party.

Dallan sat and watched the sunset, pondering his friend's advice. It was an interesting suggestion, to be sure. But even if he wasn't still furious with her, he doubted he'd go through with it.

If he found out her reasoning, that would open the door to forgiving her. And if he forgave her, well, what would stop him from wanting her all over again?

Nay, Dallan decided, standing to join the rest of the village in the feasting hall for dinner, he wasn't interested in forgiving Niamh. He just wanted to avoid her.

CHAPTER NINE

N OT ONE BELL toll later, Dallan stood in a dim corner of the cramped solar at Thurles, glaring at Niamh. He had been unable to avoid her for even that long, which did not bode well for the coming days.

She stared into the leaping flames of the hearth, far too large for a room this size, the warm firelight dancing across her face. His chest ached as he watched her, as though every time he saw her, she broke his heart anew. It hurt even more, he decided, that she was as beautiful as he remembered. Perhaps more so.

Out of morbid curiosity, he tried to spy the ring on her finger again, but her hands were folded in her lap, hiding her fingers.

Cormac stood before the small window, situated on the wall opposite the door, gazing into the cool autumn night. Heavy silence filled the air as they awaited Diarmid and Brona. Cormac had ordered Diarmid to watch the queen, who had proven uncooperative thus far. She tolerated Diarmid, but Dallan wagered she'd soon realize she was being followed, not indulged, if she hadn't already.

The door flew open. Brona strode in, her shoulders pulled back and head held high. She wore a thin golden circlet atop her dark hair. Diarmid followed her in, looking much in need of a drink.

Dallan could use one himself.

The queen sat in one of the chairs next to the fire, her back straight as a board. "Did we not already meet this morn?" she asked, looking to Cormac with raised brows. "How can there already be more to discuss?"

"Your villagers are wandering out of the fortifications," Cormac replied evenly.

"They are rebuilding their homes, taking stock of the wreckage of their lives. You would have them do nothing?"

Cormac walked away from the window to sit in the chair opposite her. "They are going into the forest to collect wood."

"A necessary step in rebuilding," the queen shot back.

Dallan hoped that Cormac's complaint was headed somewhere, for at this point he couldn't help but agree with Brona's reasoning. Yet his friend was among the wisest and most responsible men he'd ever met. Cormac did nothing without just cause, especially irritating a powerful queen.

"I agree." Cormac's deep voice was guarded. "Even if they were gathering wood for the purpose of building, I would insist on setting up greater measures for their protection. But they are piling the wood atop a small hill along the edge of the village. As though they are setting up a bonfire."

"Samhain is just over a sennight away," Brona said. "They are starting the preparations."

"Do you recall my specific instruction *not* to leave the walls of the keep until I can assure the security of the borders? I apologize if the direction was unclear. It was meant for everyone, not just the royal family."

Dallan had nothing but respect for Cormac's restraint. He would've taken that opportunity to comment on Brona's misplaced priorities, at the very least. Dallan watched Brona, by some miracle, sit even taller. He glanced at Niamh, who stared down at her hands and looked thoroughly uncomfortable at the entire situation. She had never had the patience for politics or the subtle battles of the nobility. It appeared in that, at least, she had not changed.

"Am I not the queen in these halls? Was I not given the task of overseeing the rebuilding of the village? As the village lay outside the walls of the keep and I have no sorcerer to speak of, how do you propose we build it without leaving?"

Cormac's jaw tightened noticeably, but he controlled his words. "I am responsible for your safety, and that of your people. If you cannot follow my orders regarding risk, I cannot keep you and your people safe."

The queen appeared unshaken. "You still have yet to tell me what it is you think I ought to do."

"Set up temporary shelters for folk within the bounds of the keep proper. Let them sleep in the hall, the church, the courtyard if you must. If anyone has need to leave the keep, I should be informed in advance so as to put together an escort. I realize this feels extreme, as though I overstep my reach, but it is only temporary. Once we are assured that Aodh's men have fled back to the north, you will of course be free to move about as you did before."

"He won't be coming back," Brona told him sharply. "I don't see what all the concern is over."

Dallan couldn't keep his thoughts to himself after such an outrageous statement. "Do you not see the smoke rising from your village? It has been but hours since your lives were threatened. How can you not be concerned over your safety?"

"He gave me his word." For the first time since she entered, her voice dropped noticeably.

"With respect, my lady, at this moment I'm not certain I would take Aodh at his word." Cormac's quiet tone matched her own.

Brona's eyes fell to her hands for but a moment before she looked back to Cormac. "He gave me his word, in exchange for my daughter."

Silence descended. Naught but the sound of the crackling logs in the hearth dared comment as yet.

Niamh looked up from her hands, her mouth agape.

Shifting uncomfortably, the queen continued, louder this time. "He swore that if Cara accompanied him back north, no more harm would befall Thurles. And I will not have you believe that I forced such a thing on my daughter. I am no monster. The choice was hers. Now," she declared, "may I be permitted to run *my* home as *I* see fit?"

Dallan was equally appalled and impressed. Either the woman was made of stone or her heart was, perhaps both.

"Aye," Cormac replied, "so long as you follow my guidelines for your safety. I will not rely on the word of a raiding king to determine the movements of our men. When the Fianna return, then we will decide. Until then, no one leaves the walls. Diarmid can see to any further concerns you might have."

Diarmid gave his elder brother a look that expressed precisely how he felt about his assignment.

Dallan grinned at him wickedly, earning a glare of his own.

"Niamh," Cormac called, drawing Dallan's immediate attention, "I had hoped you could report on the dead and injured. How went the day? How many were lost?"

The beauty before him drew a long, sad breath. He knew why her face looked so grim. He had heard the screams outside the infirmary.

"Ninety-seven souls lived in this village yesterday," she began. "Today, forty-two sleep in the hall, eighteen in the infirmary, and twenty-two in the ground. Fifteen I have not seen since this morn."

"You have a mind for figures?" Diarmid asked, clearly impressed.

Dallan rolled his eyes, shoving away a pang of jealousy. Of course, he would be vying for her attention. As he did with every woman he met.

"My father was a merchant," Niamh told him. "He taught me to keep ledgers."

"Will the infirm recover?" Cormac asked.

"Most will," she replied, "but several injuries are quite severe. It is too early to tell for them. My lord, there is something else I wish to discuss, if I may."

Cormac nodded for her to continue. Diarmid leaned forward in interest. Dallan forced himself to stop glaring at his friend. It wasn't as though she were his anymore.

"My supplies are running low, and if I am to continue treating the injured to the best of my ability, I will need to collect more herbs from outside the keep."

"You didn't have stock in your cottage?" Dallan asked skeptically. He could see where this was headed, and he would do everything to prevent it.

"My cottage was ransacked," she ground out, her lips tight as she turned to give him a meaningful look. "You saw it happen yourself. My shelves overturned, most of my stores destroyed. And I would still need to leave the keep to retrieve what remains."

"We will arrange it," Cormac agreed. "Is this something you do often?"

Niamh nodded. "Every few days, especially with so many patients."

Dallan shook his head imperceptibly as Cormac's eyes caught his.

"As you are one of her patients and, until today, a capable warrior, you will act as her guard whenever she needs to leave the keep."

Dallan's eyes closed in resignation. He knew Cormac did this to punish him for lack of focus. Possibly for his sour comment toward Niamh as well. Cormac had no way to know why Dallan ought to be furious with the healer.

He looked toward her, the woman who still haunted him.

But she avoided his gaze.

CHAPTER TEN

B Y DAWN THE following morn, Niamh could barely stand. She'd been tired following the attack yesterday, drained from the exertion of defending her home and family. Not to mention the shock of seeing Dallan again on top of all that. Then, after hours of treating patients, she'd been forced to sit in on the most uncomfortable meeting in the history of the kingdom.

Queen Brona had been nothing but kind to Niamh and her family. She wanted to believe that Brona had told the truth, that Cara had willingly sacrificed herself to prevent further bloodshed. Yet something felt off.

If that were true, then why wouldn't the queen have told the men so before they left and spared them the trouble?

It mattered not. Such politics were far beyond her understanding, and she had no use for them. Especially after spending much of the night in the infirmary trying to keep Tadhg alive. She'd had to take his leg off, a nightmare she'd not soon forget, and he'd been struck with fever.

Gathering her supplies once more, Niamh steeled herself for the inevitable. She'd put off checking Dallan's wound until the very last. She had no desire to see such hatred toward her in the eyes of the man she loved.

Oh, aye, Niamh had never stopped loving Dallan. She'd admitted it to herself long ago. That was why she'd left him. She knew he deserved better than she could give, and that he was stubborn enough to keep her around anyway.

Even in the midst of her work and weary to the bone, Niamh knew the moment he'd appeared outside the infirmary to wait for her. His presence set all her senses aflame.

Linens in one hand, herbs in the other, she prepared for battle and stepped out the door.

He glared at her, the pain in his eyes driving the dagger of guilt deeper. Sitting motionless and bare-chested, he looked like a work of art, a statue of one of the masters. She couldn't help but notice that he had filled out in the years since they'd parted. His muscles were no longer those of the boy she once knew, but of the man she'd broken.

She kneeled before him, reaching for the linen wrapping his wound, careful not to touch anything else.

He watched her every move.

More than anything, Niamh wanted to fall back into his arms, tell him everything and apologize until he believed her. To pretend like nothing was wrong with her.

But he deserved better than that.

Instead, she was compelled to ask him a question to which she knew he'd take exception.

"Have you been using your shoulder?"

"Yes, I fought in battle yesterday," he replied coolly.

"Have you been using your shoulder *since you were wounded?*"

"No. I've been doing just as the healer bid me."

Niamh very much doubted that. "Your wound is seeping. Which means you've been moving it too much."

"What would you have me do, Woman? Sit in front of the hearth all day?" he asked, his irritation obvious. "And if your scheme of foraging for herbs was some poor effort to try to win back my affections—"

Niamh had had enough. She'd put up with his comments until now because she knew she deserved them, but she couldn't let him start getting any ridiculous notions of her intentions.

"I'm going to stop you right there," she interrupted. "I have no interest in being anything to you other than your healer. And when that's finished, so are we."

"That statement would hurt more if you hadn't used it already," he growled.

"I wasn't trying to hurt you!" Niamh shouted in frustration.

He leaned close to her, so close she could feel the warmth of his breath on her skin. "Then what were you trying to do?" he whispered, his voice dangerous.

"Help you." The words barely escaped her lips. She sat back, putting as much distance between them as she could and while still being able to tend to him.

"Well, maybe if you told me how it is you think you're helping, I would understand."

"I'm changing the bandage on your wound and adding fresh herbs."

"That's not what I meant, and you know it," he muttered.

Of course she knew it. But she refused to be pulled into that conversation.

"And I don't understand why you're making this injury out to be more than it is," he added grumpily. "'Tis little more than a scratch."

Niamh leveled him a put-upon look. "Men can die of scratches if they are poorly tended."

"How soon 'till this is over? When will I be able to stop seeing you?"

Her heart sank at his words. "Do you think I want this? Do you think I relish coming here and enduring your fury, your disdain, every time you see me?"

"Then put me out of my misery," he begged. "Tell me why you left. At least do that much."

Niamh swallowed, willing herself to look away before she did something stupid. "I cannot. And we are going to be spending much of our time together in the coming days, so can we please try to reach some sort of compromise?"

"You mean pretend like we're friends? I can't just forget—" He couldn't finish the sentence. Niamh saw the struggle as he held back whatever had crossed his mind. She didn't want to imagine what he might have said.

"I mean stop acting like enemies. I don't expect you to be my friend, but we will make a rule. No talking about our past. Only about what's happening now. Agreed?"

He did not look pleased with her suggestion, but he nodded nonetheless.

"Now then," Niamh continued, donning a mask of happiness and ignoring the jabs of guilt that wouldn't leave her be, "about those herbs. Are you ready to leave now to gather them? It will take several hours."

Dallan narrowed one eye, deep in thought. "What if," he said, as though she hadn't spoken at all, "you tell Cormac that I'm not fit to guard you because it will impede my shoulder from healing?"

"It won't," she muttered, "as long as we aren't actually attacked. And would he really think better of you for it? Look, just help me and I swear I won't come anywhere near you, aside from when we must work together."

"Well, let's get this over with then." Dallan stood after she fastened his bandage, putting his *léine* back on and covering his impressive upper half.

It had been a *long* time since Niamh had admired a man's chest, and it didn't surprise her in the least that Dallan was the man to attract her interest. As she followed Dallan toward the castle gates, Niamh decided that she would allow herself to savor these few days she had with him as he healed. Even in his frustration with her over her continued reticence, she could tuck away a handful of memories.

After all, it would likely be the last time she saw him.

CHAPTER ELEVEN

DALLAN'S INSTINCTS WARNED him of danger. He knew absolutely nothing about this woman save that she held the power to break his heart all over again. Yet, somehow he still couldn't stop himself from admiring everything about her, from wondering what thoughts crossed her mind as she wandered beneath the trees.

Niamh's golden braids fell over her shoulders every time she bent to inspect a plant. Beneath the orange-gold canopy of the autumn woods, she glowed with warmth and light.

A misleading image, if ever Dallan saw one. In his experience, she was colder than a lake in the depths of winter. Nevertheless, she continued to draw him in, whether intentional or not.

Dallan followed her through the brush, far off any pathway, as she picked and plucked her way through the first flush of fallen leaves. She wore a plain brown gown, fitted but not tight. She'd not spoken a word to him since they'd left Thurles, over an hour ago now. Lost in his thoughts, Dallan hadn't realized he'd been staring at her until she bent to pick another herb, her dress hugging her curves as she reached down.

Then it all came back to him.

The feel of her soft skin beneath his hands.

Her laughter at the kitten's antics.

The delicious sounds she made as he pleasured her.

How damned good it felt to be inside her.

He swore under his breath, willing his mind to cease its torture.

Dallan shut his eyes tightly, hoping to blink away the memory of her. He'd managed to live the past six years without her tormenting his every thought. He could continue to do so.

At his outburst, Niamh stood and turned to him. "What is it?" Genuine worry threaded her words. "Did you see someone? Is there danger?"

"Nay," he answered, finding a tree a good distance away from her. He didn't trust himself to be near her at the moment.

"Then what's the matter?"

"Nothing." What could he say? That he'd been so struck by the memory of their lovemaking that he could barely conceal it? Aye, she'd take that well.

Her pale brown brows furrowed. Adorably.

Damnit.

"Is it your shoulder?" she pressed. "Let me take a look." She rushed over to him, as though he were ready to fall dead to the ground.

"I'm fine." He moved quickly from the tree, putting even more space between them. "What are you looking for? Perhaps I can be of some assistance."

It was better than what he'd been doing, anyway.

She stopped, considering him. "Very well." She pulled a stem out of her basket with several leaves and blackberries on it. "Are you familiar with blackberries?"

"With eating them, aye."

She gave him a look that, six years ago, would have had him pulling her in for a kiss.

Now, it made him grimace in frustration.

"I need the leaves and whatever berries are left. If you can hunt for these, I can find some of the other herbs I need. They like a lot of light, so they aren't as common in the deep woods, but you might find a few. I often see them just outside stands of pine." She walked right up to him, holding out the stem she'd grabbed from her basket.

The smell of lavender—of *her*—surrounded him, taking him prisoner and threatening the last shreds of his self-control. He needed to get away from her. Quickly.

After dutifully listening to her explanation of how to identify the plant, he hurried away in search of the nearest stand of pines.

And his sanity.

DALLAN WAS BEHAVING…ODDLY. Niamh couldn't decide what felt off, so she set about searching for as many of the herbs on her long list as she could find. Unfortunately, with the weather chilling and autumn upon them, she'd have to make it through the winter without many of the staples she normally stocked. She hoped to find a few late bloomers, but it was unlikely she'd forage enough to fully replenish her supply.

The sun hung halfway to the western horizon when Dallan returned with an armful of thorn-covered brambles.

"I should have given you the basket." She hurried over to take them from him. "Your arms will be scratched."

The piercing look he gave her left her breathless.

It was the way he always looked before he kissed her.

Niamh no longer wondered at his odd behavior. His chestnut eyes told her everything. "I'm sorry," she whispered.

"I can handle a few scratches." His soft reply matched her own.

"Not for the brambles." She swallowed, pressing on before she lost her nerve. "I'm sorry I hurt you." So much for not talking about their past.

His jaw clenched, but he said nothing, his stare still boring into her soul.

Niamh looked away, unable to maintain her composure as he stirred up feelings she'd long let lie. Love. Hope. Joy. Desire.

She didn't deserve any of them.

Instead, she tore the leaves and berries from the long, prickly branches, not making a sound as the thorns bit into her fingers.

Dallan kneeled down to do the same.

"Is someone pursuing you?" he asked, startling her.

Niamh looked around the clearing, and he almost smiled. She saw the corners of his mouth lift before he resumed his usual melancholy.

"You needn't worry." His husky voice sent a shiver of desire through her, reminding her of a time long since gone. "You're safe. I meant is anyone pursuing you *romantically*."

A flush rose to her cheeks.

"You said we could discuss the present," he reminded her before she could protest his intrusive question.

"No," she admitted quietly.

Her answer appeared to unsettle him. "Really?"

"No one has in years." She didn't explain that it was by her own design, that she wore his ring, in part, to keep men at a distance, lest she disappoint them as well. The reasoning mattered not. She tore another leaf from the pile.

"So there was someone?" His voice took on a hard edge.

She glared at him. He knew he was breaking their truce, treading on dangerous ground.

"Not...*then*," he grumbled. "After."

Niamh pressed her lips together, uncertain of whether she should indulge this particular question.

"I'll make a deal with you," she told him several moments later. "I'll answer your question if you answer mine."

"Deal."

"If you must know, I haven't so much as kissed anyone in the past six years. Happy?" Unable to sit still any longer, Niamh grabbed what remained of the brambles and shoved them into her basket, picking it up and waiting for him to follow.

Daring a glance, she saw the sparkle of mischief in his eyes—something she never thought she'd glimpse again. When he caught her looking, he grinned wickedly, the same grin that once had made her heart do flips and her stomach flutter. She ignored the fact that it apparently still worked.

"A bit," he admitted. "Worried no one could live up to me?"

She knew he jested by his tone. He had no idea how near the truth he'd struck.

Niamh didn't doubt for a moment that she'd never find another man like Dallan.

"My turn," she evaded. "Why did you leave in such a rush earlier?"

The smile faded from his face. "What do you mean?"

"Just before you left to find the blackberries. I thought something was upsetting you, and then you ran off in a hurry. I just wondered what was bothering you."

Dallan walked over to her, stopping so close his arm brushed hers. A shock like lightning erupted through her from the place where they touched.

"Do you really want to know?"

Niamh knew that tone. Her body reacted treacherously, though her good sense held her steady. Against her better judgment, she nodded.

He leaned down, his hot breath warming her ear as he whispered. "I couldn't stop thinking about having you naked in my arms again. I thought you'd appreciate it if I kept my hands to myself."

Taking the heavily laden basket from her, Dallan strode ahead, looking entirely too pleased with himself. For several moments, it was all Niamh could do to catch her breath as her heart raced like an arrow toward its target.

CHAPTER TWELVE

I T HAD BEEN a low blow, thrusting old emotions on her, teasing her with some of their best memories, especially after they'd agreed not to bring it up.

But, in his defense, she'd asked. And his answer, though provocative, had been truthful.

His heart might have built barriers to keep her far away, where she could do less damage, but his body betrayed him at every turn, reminding him how deeply he still desired her.

The following morn, he headed to the infirmary after he broke his fast, reminding himself that he *was not* eager to see her again.

Hopefully he'd believe it before he arrived.

When he opened the door to the modest stone building, Dallan didn't know what to expect. Would she be angry? Would she finally be honest? Would she throw herself into his arms but leave him guessing? Perhaps nothing would have changed at all.

The one possibility he hadn't considered was that he should find her in a crumpled heap, bent in half over her worktable and sobbing uncontrollably. Rushing over, he took her into his arms without a second thought.

She soaked his *léine* with her tears as he rubbed her back, sniffling and hiccoughing, unable to take a full breath.

At first Dallan worried his comment last eve had rattled her, but even if it had, she'd not be in such a state now. She'd have shed her tears last night, maybe, but he knew she'd not let him see it.

Not if it had anything to do with him.

Searching the room as he held her shaking body, Dallan finally identified the problem. On a cot nearby, a man missing one leg had the ashen pallor of death. Dallan had fought enough battles to know the unmistakable look of it when he saw it.

Smoothing her disheveled hair, he did his best to soothe her.

"I'm sorry, Niamh," he whispered into her hair, ignoring the overpowering scent of lavender that accompanied his every breath.

"I lost him," she managed, sucking in a ragged breath. "I couldn't stop his fever. Nothing worked."

Dallan took her gently by the shoulders, pulling back to look her dead in the eyes. "You did your best. He was lucky to have you with him."

"I failed him."

His heart ached at the look on her face. "You are the best healer in all of Éire, and I won't hear otherwise. If you couldn't save him, he wasn't meant to be saved."

She threw herself back into his arms. She yet shook, but her tears abated. "I've never lost a patient to aught but old age."

Dallan squeezed her tight, as though he could push all her sadness and grief from her in one giant embrace. "Have you healed men wounded in battle before?"

She stood quiet for so long he thought she wouldn't answer. When finally she spoke, her voice was stronger. "Yes, but not like this. They had walked for several days back home."

"Then you tended those with the least grievous wounds. His death is not your burden to bear."

A woman cleared her throat behind them, startling both Dallan and Niamh. Dallan turned to see Niamh's mother, Líadan, standing wide-eyed holding the cat in her arms. Morrígan looked none too pleased to be there. Before Líadan could say a word, Morrígan meowed in irritation and forced herself free from Líadan's grasp.

"How is your shoulder coming along?" she asked, kindly ignoring that she'd caught them in a rather familiar embrace.

"Much better, thank you." Dallan turned to Niamh. "How can I help?"

Líadan, apparently just noticing the streaks on Niamh's cheeks from her profusion of tears, rushed to her daughter's side. "What's happened?" She looked at Dallan accusingly before turning back to Niamh. "Sweetheart?"

Dallan couldn't help but feel a tad sour about being the first place she looked for trouble. Hadn't her daughter been the one to leave him? What did the woman think he had done?

"Tadhg...died." Niamh tripped over the last word, her tears springing anew.

"Oh, honey." Líadan pulled her into a hug, comforting her as only a mother could. "I'll have Máire help me clean him and wrap him. Don't you think on it anymore." When Niamh's sobs grew stronger, Líadan held her daughter's face so they stared at one another. "Now you listen here. It is not your fault. You did your best. And now Tadhg can join his family. Surely, that's what he'd have wanted."

Dallan couldn't stand to see Niamh so beset. She'd always had a kind heart. He knew she would take such a blow harder than most.

"You stay with her while I fetch Máire," Líadan ordered Dallan with a pointed look, hurrying from the infirmary without waiting for his reply.

"Where is his family buried?" Dallan ventured.

"In the graveyard at the church." Niamh wiped her eyes.

"I'll dig a grave for him."

She perked up at that. "You shouldn't. Your shoulder—"

"Is fully healed. As I said, it was just a scratch. Go on, inspect it for yourself." He took off his *léine*, sitting on a bench beside her worktable so that she could see his shoulder easily.

"You're right." Niamh looked up at him, a single tear falling down her cheek. "You don't need to see me anymore."

Against his better judgment, Dallan brushed it away with his finger.

And she fell into his arms again, her tears returning anew.

NIAMH'S DAY PASSED her by in a blur. She'd stayed awake the entire night, fighting to save Tadhg's life. Even when it was clear she was losing the battle, she persevered. But as the hours passed, his body only grew hotter, sweat pouring from his brow by midnight. In the darkest hours of the night, his arm went putrid. Still she washed, applied poultices, administered infusions.

By daybreak, she'd lost him. It happened so quickly. The shock lasted for some time, until just before Dallan arrived. By that point, between exhaustion and anger and grief and a thousand other horrid feelings, she could do naught but release it all.

She hardly remembered their exchange, except that he'd been incredibly kind and comforted her. Her mother and Máire had come by with Alva, who had brought her to the kitchens for a meal.

As she lay in her bed, Morrígan purring contentedly on her stomach, Niamh reached into the depths of her mind, trying to recall what Dallan had said to her. She remembered the warmth of his body, the strength of his arms about her, the soft lilt of his deep voice comforting her.

Her door cracked open and her mother smiled at her, stepping in and sitting on the bed beside her. "You should be resting."

"Spoken like a mother," Niamh retorted with a small smile.

"I want to talk to you, but if you need rest first then it can wait."

Niamh sat up, earning a loud protest from Morrígan. Her mother rarely sounded so serious. "What is it? Is something wrong? Is someone else sick?"

She began pushing the covers off her, but her mother stayed her hand.

"We need to speak of Dallan."

Niamh inhaled sharply. "There's little to say. Now that he's healed, I won't be seeing him again."

Her mother looked down at her own lap, her hands resting on Niamh's. "I don't think that's true. And I think you know it as well."

Against her better judgment, Niamh *hoped* to see Dallan again, but she would hardly say that qualified as knowing that she would.

"Or," her mother continued, "perhaps you are less observant than I thought."

"He's furious with me," Niamh reminded her mother. "Even if I saw him a hundred more times, there'd still be nothing to speak of, save the ferocity of his mood."

"Oh, honey. The way he's been looking at you, if you saw him a hundred more times he'd ask for your hand all over again."

Niamh's breath stilled, her hands going cold. "He's only being nice because we agreed not to discuss our past. The moment it comes up, he'll be as cold as he was before. And for good reason."

Her mother nodded slowly, as though giving her words consideration. "Be that as it may, I feel obligated as your mother to make a suggestion."

Niamh's stomach dropped. She knew what was coming. She knew the right thing to do. "Never see him again. I know."

"The opposite, actually."

Niamh looked up at her mother, confused. "What do you mean?"

"You have been so quiet, so sad, since that day all those years ago. Why not give yourself the chance for a better life? Why not tell him your secret and let him decide? I know you still love him."

"You know I can't."

"You *can*," her mother pressed, "and I think you *should*. Not for him, for you. The worst that could happen is he agrees with you and you remain unmarried, but at least you'd know for certain. You could move on with your life."

"The worst that could happen is he tells me it matters not, that he doesn't want children, and the fact that I can't have any doesn't change how he feels. Because then I would marry him. And when he realized I meant it, that I wasn't imagining it or misunderstanding my condition, when he *finally* understood he would never have any heirs to his kingdom, he would leave me."

Her mother pulled her into her arms, squeezing her shoulders in a tight hug. "Dallan is a better man than your father," she whispered. "I don't think he would leave."

Niamh pulled away to face her mother. "Then he would take a second wife, as Alva's husband will if she doesn't conceive soon. Or his family would declaim the marriage for lack of heirs. There is no good ending."

Her mother patted her hand gently then stood, a frown creasing the lines on her face. "It's your mistake to make. But you know my thinking on the matter. Now get some rest."

Niamh pulled Morrígan to lay on her chest, petting her soft, tickly fur. For most of her life, she'd taken the advice her mother offered. But this? It was ridiculous.

Of course, she wished she could just tell Dallan everything, marry him, and live happily together.

But Niamh knew life wasn't really like the ballads sung by the bards. Allowing herself to believe otherwise was a certain path to a shattered heart.

Her father had more than proven that.

CHAPTER THIRTEEN

THE FOLLOWING MORN, Dallan inhaled his oat bread and hard cheese, grabbing a handful of smoked salmon and two apples as he stood, preparing to rush to the infirmary. Cormac's hard stare and Diarmid's mocking smile stopped him in his tracks.

"What?" he demanded.

Cormac shook his head, apparently choosing not to comment, and turned back to his own meal.

Diarmid nodded toward the pair of apples. "Off to proclaim your love, are you? Won't that enchanting healer know what apples symbolize?"

"Shall I bring her your bread instead, then?" Dallan growled in response. He'd learned his lesson the last time he'd proclaimed his love to that particular healer. It wasn't an experience he cared to repeat anytime soon.

Diarmid sat back from his meal, crossing his arms and regarding Dallan thoughtfully. "What's with you and this woman? You're behaving strangely."

Cormac looked back up.

Dallan shifted his weight as the two brothers inspected him closer than he liked. "I need to get to the infirmary. Are you ladies done yet?"

"You haven't shown any interest in a woman the entire time I've known you," Cormac observed at last, ignoring Dallan's impatience.

"I heard a rumor," Diarmid began with a confident smirk,

"that you already knew Niamh. From long ago."

Dallan did his best not to react, to keep his face unreadable. He knew he'd failed when Diarmid's smirk grew to a haughty grin and Cormac's eyes narrowed.

"Sit." Cormac ordered.

"But—"

"I'm your commander." The subtle smile forming to match his brother's signaled to Dallan that his commander was about to abuse his power.

Dallan glared at him as he returned to his seat next to Diarmid.

"Are you really going to make us ask?" Diarmid looked positively giddy. He was as bad a gossip as any of the household servants. Likely he had overheard one of them talking.

"I fell in love with her when we were but children. She left me. That's all there is to it."

"That's not all," Diarmid argued.

"Why would you think I'm lying?"

"You're not lying," Cormac answered. "But in situations such as these, the information offered is *never* all of it."

Diarmid was nodding emphatically. "You may as well tell us now. We can always just ask Niamh."

Dallan groaned in frustration. "Fine. I courted her for a year and when I proposed she said no, left the village, and I never saw her again. Until we arrived here."

"Did she tell you why?" Diarmid pressed.

Dallan simply shook his head.

"Unacceptable."

"For once I agree with you," Dallan replied to Diarmid. "Which is why there's nothing going on. I don't know why she wouldn't marry me then and she still won't tell me now."

"If she's rebuffed you twice over, why are you running to take her apples and salmon?" Cormac, ever the voice of reason, questioned.

"Finn suggested winning back some of her trust so that she'll finally tell me what happened, and I can stop wondering. And she had a hard day yesterday. I want to check on her. I can be nice to her without trying to get her into my bed, can't I?"

Diarmid said, "No," at the same time as Cormac nodded in agreement. As they looked at each other, preparing for a debate, Dallan used the opportunity to finally get out of the hall and over to the infirmary.

Though he wasn't thrilled that two more people knew his embarrassing tale, he felt somewhat vindicated that they also thought she should have offered a reason for her rejection.

But now was not the time to dwell on the past. Niamh needed a friend, not a vengeful past lover. Today, he would put aside any bitterness and support her.

Dallan strode through the open doors, preparing himself for a repeat of yesterday, when he'd found Niamh crying her heart out. He was relieved when he sighted her laying out blackberry leaves to dry.

She looked up at him, her honey-colored eyes sunken, shadows forming beneath them. Half of her flaxen hair had escaped from her braids. She was exhausted.

"Did you sleep?" he asked, walking over and setting one of the apples and all of the salmon on the table in front of her.

"Good morning to you, too," she replied with a sharp look, eyeing the food he'd brought.

"And yes, I did sleep." She picked up a strip of salmon and took a bite, looking up at him with a weak smile. "Thank you. It's delicious."

"You're welcome. And you didn't sleep enough. Why don't you go lie down? Perhaps I can…" he gestured broadly to the table where she was working, "help?"

She laughed once, the sound a lightning strike of memory.

"I like it when you laugh."

"You have a way of bringing it about."

Dallan took a bite of his apple, refusing to back down. "Really, you should rest more. I can see how hard you've been working." He looked around the room, spotting only two patients remaining of her original eighteen. They slumbered peacefully, neither seeming in critical condition. "They'll be fine without you. I can stay here and keep an eye on things if you'd like."

Niamh narrowed her eyes at him. "You're too persuasive for your own good."

"Does that mean you will?"

"Yes, I will go lie down. Happy?"

Dallan took another bite of his apple and grinned at her. "Very."

"Niamh?"

Dallan turned to see a woman he didn't recognize walking hurriedly into the infirmary, her harried gaze fixed on Niamh.

"Alva? What's the matter?" Niamh rushed over to the woman, who quickly whispered something.

Dallan's first instinct was to excuse himself, as Alva clearly desired a private word with Niamh. He stayed, however, because he still intended to see Niamh sent to rest. Instead of leaving, he turned toward the table, focusing his attention on the herbs laid out there as he finished his apple.

Several moments later, Alva left as swiftly as she'd arrived and Niamh returned to pick up another piece of salmon.

"Is she alright?"

"She's run out of the infusion I made for her." Niamh grabbed a leather bag with her free hand, peeking inside and frowning.

"And you don't have what you need to make more for her?"

Niamh shook her head, her eyes taking on a faraway cast, her face even more pale than it had been.

"Can I take you to get more?"

"I doubt it," she muttered, setting down the bag and the salmon. "I had to place a special order with the merchant, and it took him weeks to find the ingredients. I don't know where I'd get them quickly enough to help her." Now she began pacing before the table, one hand on her forehead.

"What are the ingredients?"

"Cinnamon and oranges," she replied absently, her mind far afield.

Damn. He didn't know what he'd expected, but he'd hoped it was something he could help her find. It didn't matter, though. He hated seeing her so upset, two days in a row now. "I'll see what I can do, but only if you promise me you'll rest."

Niamh spun toward him. "You think you could find them?"

Dallan moved closer to her. "I don't know, but I'll do what I can to help. Don't get too excited just yet."

For the second time in as many days, Niamh threw herself into his arms. This time, however, it was so unexpected he had to take a step backwards to avoid falling. He had no idea what was wrong with Niamh's friend, but if it was this important to her, Dallan would do everything he could to help.

After seeing Niamh's struggles to keep the villagers alive and healthy, after realizing the toll it took on her, it was clear she needed a friend of her own.

Or, at the very least, a determined past lover who was prepared to look out for her.

CHAPTER FOURTEEN

Niamh's world continued to spin further and further off course. She felt as though she were living some strange, alternate life, where only the most unexpected things occurred.

First, Dallan had appeared, acting as though they were the best of friends with no bad blood between them. Had he truly forgiven her? He couldn't have. Even she hadn't forgiven herself for breaking his heart. Perhaps he still pitied her over the loss of Tadhg. No matter his motives, Dallan's kindness toward her had breathed new life into her day.

Until Alva arrived.

Niamh's stomach turned just thinking about it.

Alva had worked hard to keep from tearing up as she confided that her husband had sat down with her the night prior and told her he wanted to take a second wife. Alva recounted the heartbreaking conversation, beating herself up over her inability to give him any children at all. Niamh felt that pain as though it were her own. If things had gone differently, it could have been. Further proof that she'd made the right decision.

In spite of all of it, Alva was determined to give her husband a child. Except that she had run out of the infusion of cinnamon and bitter orange. She'd been using it regularly, and it hadn't lasted as long as Niamh had expected.

Now, it all fell to Niamh.

And she wouldn't let Alva down.

The trouble was that the merchant had been killed in the raid, and Niamh wasn't allowed to leave the keep, let alone undertake some overland journey in search of rare ingredients for a woman who was otherwise in good health.

She shuffled again through the sparse selection of herbs and berries she'd managed to collect while foraging with Dallan. She needed to have him take her back out. They hadn't even collected enough to hold over the village through the winter.

And none of it would help Alva.

Niamh sighed. Dallan had said he might be able to help, so that was something. And she'd promised him she would get some rest. She should probably go lie down before he commented on her fretting. Leaving the infirmary only a few short hours after arriving, Niamh crossed the courtyard toward the room she shared with her mother and Máire.

So few had survived, that between the hall and the empty rooms of the keep and its outbuildings, everyone had a pallet for themselves—some more private than others. How she longed to be back in her little cottage, with her warm quilted blanket and a crackling fire. It wasn't for lack of solitude, though.

Niamh had been sharing a room with her mother for much of her adult life, ever since her father had left shortly after they moved away from Nás. He'd always been so happy, so warm, so talkative. Niamh had no idea anything was wrong until one morn she woke and he was gone. He hadn't even waited to say goodbye to her. According to her mother, he hadn't wanted to explain to Niamh why he was leaving.

The irony of that had stung almost as much as his absence.

Lost in her thoughts, Brona and Catrin, the queen's youngest daughter, surprised her when they appeared in her path.

"Niamh!" Brona greeted her cheerily. "How are you, my dear? How are you faring after all this disruption?"

"As well as can be expected, I suppose."

"How are the injured doing? Do you have everything you need to care for them?"

Niamh perked up at that. "Well, actually, I've run out of quite a few supplies. I was permitted to forage a few days ago, but—"

"Well, it seems today is your lucky day," Brona interrupted. Catrin and I were just headed down into the village to take stock of the situation. Why don't you join us? We can see if any of your stockpile survived the fire."

A weight that Niamh hadn't realized she'd carried lifted from her shoulders. "Really?"

"Of course. It'd be no trouble at all. Not even out of the way."

"But my cottage is—was—on the edge of the village."

Brona took Niamh's arm, leading her toward the gate. "We need to inspect the entire village, including the area around your cottage."

Niamh's sudden surge of hope overtook her good sense for only a moment. As they approached the guard tower at the front gate, Niamh remembered that no one was to leave the village unguarded. Cormac had made that quite clear.

"Brona," Niamh ventured hesitantly. One did not often question a queen. "What about Cormac's orders? Shouldn't we have a guard come with us? I could probably—"

"No need to worry over that," she interrupted. "He's already agreed to it."

Niamh looked from Brona to Catrin, who glared at her mother reproachfully. Something told Niamh that Cormac had no idea that Brona planned to leave the keep today.

She should excuse herself. Claim exhaustion and promise to accompany them another time. Thank the queen for her generous offer.

In any other situation, she would have done precisely that. But this was different.

Because inside her cottage, she had stores of cinnamon and orange.

THE VILLAGE BEFORE them lay in shambles, a charcoal wasteland of indistinguishable remnants of lives now lost. Three buildings had been mercifully spared, easily spotted against the razed horizon. Her cottage wasn't one of them.

The three women stood side by side, surrounded by destruction. Brona clicked her tongue in disapproval, as though Aodh were a lad who'd misbehaved and not a grown man who'd burned their village to the ground.

"I can't believe he'd do such a thing," Brona proclaimed sadly.

Catrin glared at her mother. "Don't."

"Catrin." The warning tone in Brona's voice set Niamh on edge.

Catrin opened her mouth to reply, but when her eyes met Niamh's she closed it again, fury writ on her face.

"Let's have a look around, shall we? See what damage Aodh has wrought." Brona eyed Catrin as she spoke.

Niamh found the entire exchange unsettling. "I'm going to head down to my cottage. It will take some time to go through the rubble." As she stepped down the blackened path, she heard Catrin mumble behind her.

"It's not like it was his fault."

Brona shushed her daughter loudly enough that Niamh could hear it several paces away. She wished she hadn't heard any of it.

Because now she was curious, and also obligated to tell someone that perhaps Brona and Catrin were keeping secrets about Aodh and the raid.

Disturbing secrets, if Catrin's salty comment held any grain of truth.

How could it not have been Aodh's fault? She had seen the man himself on the battlefield, leading his men, torching cottages. Determining she would think on it more later, Niamh pushed any thought of Aodh from her weary mind and focused on helping Alva.

If she hadn't known precisely what the view from her cottage looked like, Niamh would never have found it. The remains of one building ran into the next, so that she could hardly tell where her home ended and another began.

Every step she took over the crumbled threshold broke another piece of her past. Items she once loved crushed to dust beneath her feet, crying out as they disappeared forever. She spotted several spindles from the chair where her mother had sat in the corner, warring with Morrígan. To her right was a patch of fabric from the padded woolen quilt that Máire had made her. It had been a Yuletide gift, made with love for the coldest nights of the year. Niamh knew she'd spent far too much money on the materials, and a good deal of time attending the detailed stitching. There was a good reason such blankets were rare.

And in the far corner of the room, shattered, broken and scattered, lay Niamh's herbs. Fractured jars and burned-up pouches littered the ground. Reaching down, she picked up a thorn-covered stem, charred and bent. A rose.

Or what was left of one.

Deep in her gut, she knew she wouldn't be able to salvage anything. Even seeing the futility in her search, Niamh tucked up the hem of her gown, sucked in a deep breath, and began her search for cinnamon and orange.

She never found it.

CHAPTER FIFTEEN

A KNOCK SOUNDED on Dallan's door as he fastened the belt around his clean *léine*. After a day spent minding the infirmary and helping to repair the burned and broken palisade wall, Dallan had desperately needed a good washing and some fresh clothes. His belly rumbled demandingly as he opened the door to find Diarmid.

"Cormac wants us in the solar," he grumbled.

"Now?" Dallan protested. "Can't he just tell us at dinner?"

"Apparently not."

When they arrived in the solar only minutes later, they found Cormac sitting thoughtfully before the hearth, his arms across his chest.

"We have a problem," he declared. "Brona is openly defying my orders, and endangering others in the process."

"What did she do?" Diarmid asked, taking the seat opposite his brother.

"She and Catrin spent much of the afternoon down in the village. Unguarded." He turned to look at Dallan. "They took your healer with them."

Dallan's throat constricted. "She swore she'd get some rest," he grumbled. And she wasn't *his*. Not anymore.

"I just spoke with Brona, who told me Niamh believed they had some sort of approval to leave the keep."

Dallan could hardly believe it. Why would she do something so reckless? Didn't she realize they were at risk of another attack?

Until they could determine why Aodh came all the way to Thurles, specifically, the Fianna couldn't be certain he wouldn't do so again.

"I'll speak with her," Dallan promised. "I don't know what she was thinking."

"If I had to venture a guess," Cormac replied evenly, "she was thinking it unwise to defy a queen. Brona is lying to us, that much becomes clearer with each passing day. What we don't know is why."

Understanding dawned on Dallan. "You want me to ask Niamh about Brona, not censure her for leaving the keep."

"Precisely."

"Brona's position here is tenuous, and she knows it. I don't know what she's up to or why, but we need to find out. See if Niamh learned anything. If not, and you believe she can be trusted, perhaps have her try to get Brona talking. And you, little brother," Cormac turned to stare down Diarmid, "you need to follow her more closely. I'm releasing you from all your other duties. Your only job is to keep an eye on Brona."

Diarmid threw his head back against the top of the chair, with the sort of dramatic flair Dallan once loved to employ. "What of training?"

Cormac shook his head, sending Diarmid to his feet in frustration. Several choice oaths accompanied him out the door. Dallan turned to follow him.

"Dallan?"

He looked back at Cormac questioningly. "Aye?"

"Be sure Niamh knows not to take Brona at her word again. That woman cannot be trusted."

"Do you really think she could cause that much trouble?"

"No," Cormac admitted, "but I've also learned never to underestimate a queen at risk of losing her throne."

Dallan nodded his understanding. As he walked from the solar to the feasting hall, he sorted through the myriad thoughts and feelings he had on the matter. He had barely time enough to decide what to say to Niamh when he'd reached her table.

She sat in the warm light of flickering candles and fading sun, her golden hair held back in one long braid. Máire, across from her, said something that made Niamh explode into laughter.

Dallan felt a pull deep in his chest as he watched her face light up, her lips curve into a smile. He still wanted to be the one that made her laugh. In spite of all of it, he still felt as drawn to her as he had that day in the courtyard at Nás so long ago.

Niamh looked up, her mirthful gaze connecting with his own.

She took his breath away.

And she knew it, for her expression sobered after she regarded him for a moment.

Dallan strode over to the table, never taking his eyes off her. "Can I speak with you for a moment?"

Máire and Líadan went quiet. Niamh stood and followed Dallan to one of the alcoves along the edge of the room, built for precisely such a use.

Dallan had planned what he would say—something reasonable, understanding. But when she stepped closer and he caught the scent of lavender, of *her*, all sense fled him.

"You lied to me," he whispered. "You promised you'd rest."

"I'm sorry," she answered softly. "Brona intercepted me on the way to my quarters."

"She also claimed it was your idea to leave without a guard."

"What!" Niamh's cry drew the attention of the table nearby. She smiled at them, waving them away. "I was the one who offered to go find a guard. I told her it was a bad idea."

"Then why did you go?" He didn't even try to mask his concern. "What if another army had come?"

Niamh looked at her feet, shifting her weight. "Brona told me they had permission to go. It didn't make sense to me, but I went along with it because she offered to let me search through my cottage. I know that Cormac's been letting people go out to find their belongings with guards, but I've been so busy in the infirmary and—"

Dallan took her hands in his, halting her explanation. He knew why she would agree to take such a risk, given the opportunity to search the wreckage of her cottage. She'd be looking for those supplies she needed.

"Did you find them?" he asked gently.

"No. There was nothing left."

He squeezed her hands, the warmth of her touch sending chills down his arms. He swallowed back the urge to pull her in for a kiss. "A merchant came through Caiseal just before we left for Thurles. He may still be there. I can ask Cormac about taking you to see him."

Her grey eyes lit up. "Really?"

"Really. We can leave tomorrow, if he agrees." Lord help him, how could he possibly be falling for her all over again?

"I—" she began, stopping nearly as soon as she'd started.

"You can tell me, Niamh," he whispered.

And regretted it instantly. She looked about ready to cry again.

"No," she breathed, "that's just it. I can't tell you. I was going to say that I owe you, but I know what you would ask, and I can't give it to you."

"We promised not to talk about the past." He raised a hand to cup her cheek, brushing his thumb along her soft, smooth skin. "I think you're the one breaking our agreement now."

He tried to ease the pain he saw on her face but appeared to only be making matters worse.

She lifted her hand to cover his. Maybe he wasn't doing as poorly as he thought.

Desperate to ease the growing tension, Dallan changed the subject. "How about this," he ventured. "You can make it up to me by helping the Fianna and keeping it quiet."

Niamh perked up at that. "How can I help?"

Dallan scanned the room to be certain no one sat near enough to hear his hushed explanation. "We think Brona is hiding something. Cormac wants us to find out what it is."

"I think Catrin is your best bet there, but I'll do what I can."

"Catrin? She wouldn't betray her mother, even if she knew what she was hiding."

The corners of Niamh's perfect lips lifted into an adorable half-smile. "She would, I think, with enough persuading."

"What do you know that I don't? Did they say something today?"

Niamh stepped closer, her chest pressing against his own distractingly. "They had an odd sort of argument, almost silent. About Aodh."

Dallan's mind sharpened from its haze of Niamh. "Aodh? What did they say?"

"Catrin seemed to think Aodh was in the right, or that Brona wasn't judging him fairly. They both tread carefully when I was around, hardly spoke at all after that. She was *defending* him."

"But—" Dallan couldn't understand why she would possibly hold Aodh in any sort of esteem.

"I know," Niamh agreed. "You'd think she'd hold more of a grudge after he murdered her father, kidnapped her sister, and burned her village to the ground. Which is why I would start by talking with *her*."

"I'll make you a deal," Dallan offered, his lips a breath away from her forehead. "You speak with Catrin about Aodh, and I'll speak with Cormac about Caiseal."

"I think I can manage that," she replied. "Did you need any-thing else? I think they're bringing out the meal."

"I can think of a few things," he whispered, stepping back before he did something he would regret. He needed to win her trust, not turn back into the boy of nineteen who couldn't keep himself away from her. "But I'll leave you to your dinner."

Even as he reminded himself, for the hundredth time since they'd begun speaking, that she had left him, that she didn't want him, Dallan couldn't help but notice the flush in her cheeks or the sensual parting of her lips.

She may not love him, but 'twas clear to Dallan that she still desired him.

And it was a start.

CHAPTER SIXTEEN

NIAMH SWALLOWED BACK the overwhelming urge to throw herself into Dallan's arms. Again. She'd already done so too many times, and she wasn't about to put them both in danger of heartbreak. As she neared her seat, she caught pointed looks from Máire and her mother.

"What was that about?" Her mother didn't hesitate as Niamh sat down with them.

"Nothing. Dallan just wanted to be certain I was feeling better."

"Did he now?" Her mother didn't sound surprised in the least. Rather, she sounded entirely too optimistic.

"He was standing awfully close to you," Máire commented.

"He was?" Niamh pretended ignorance. "I'd hardly noticed."

"Then why are your cheeks so flushed?" Máire pressed ruthlessly.

Niamh glared at her. "It was *nothing*," she repeated.

"If you aren't careful, you'll end up in exactly the situation we left Nás to avoid. Six years later and you'll have your heart broken all the same." Máire's eyes held naught but concern, and Niamh appreciated her friend.

When it was clear Dallan would be staying in Thurles, Niamh had made Máire swear to do her utmost to keep Niamh from making the mistake of falling for his charms, of thinking with her heart instead of her mind.

"Thank you," Niamh told her. "I'll be careful."

"So what did he actually want?" her mother continued, undeterred.

Niamh grimaced, looking at Máire.

"Oh, Lord, what did you do now?" Máire hissed. "I hoped we'd be past all this once he healed."

"You know how I ran out of Alva's treatments?"

"Yes." Máire's tone indicated that she didn't know where Niamh was headed, but she knew she didn't want to go there.

"He offered to take me to Caiseal tomorrow to a merchant to see if I can find the supplies I need."

"What!" It wasn't a question.

"I think that's a wonderful idea," Niamh's mother added quietly. "You need the supplies, and it's kind of him to help."

"You know it's not the supplies he's after," Máire warned. "I should accompany you."

"You should do no such thing," her mother's tight reply surprised both Niamh and Máire. "They need to sort all this business out, one way or another, and you'd only get in the way."

"But mother," Niamh protested, "it would be unseemly."

"Did he not escort you to the forest not so long ago? How many times has he visited the infirmary while Máire or I are out? And you aren't a noble. We were close once, but even that is a distant memory. Go alone."

Máire looked ready to argue but held her tongue. Niamh opened her mouth to protest, but her mother wouldn't budge.

"Is your only objection that you fear it will end in heartbreak?" her mother questioned.

"For both of us, most likely, aye."

Her mother turned fully toward her, taking Niamh's hands in her own. Leaning forward, she whispered, "Can you not see that it already has? You risk no further injury, only the loss of future happiness. Your heart has been broken since the day we left. You deserve the chance to mend it."

Niamh inhaled a shaky breath, trying to find a way to argue with her mother.

But she couldn't.

Because, as much as it scared her to admit it, the woman had a point.

"What are you suggesting?" She could hardly believe she'd entertained the thought, let alone uttered the words.

"Tell him everything."

Niamh's stomach heaved at the idea. "I can't," she whispered back, hushing the voice in the back of her mind that added *not yet*.

"I think it akin to toying with fire." Máire's pragmatic statement broke Niamh's trance. "There's more here than just the past between you. You've been building a new relationship, pretending to be friends. It's far more complicated than it was a fortnight ago."

"Matters of the heart are both irrationally complex and devastatingly simple," her mother answered with a sad smile. "Honesty will get you to the right of it, one way or another."

Niamh knew from past experience that the pair of them could argue over her love life, or lack thereof, for hours. She hurriedly finished another bite of her stew before rising to seek out Catrin. The best way to take her mind off her own problems was to solve someone else's.

She intercepted the princess as she left the dais where the royal family dined, pulling her aside into the corridor of columns surrounding the hall.

"Would you care to join me?" Niamh asked, indicating the length of the corridor.

Catrin turned back to look at the table where her mother was finishing her dinner.

"Absolutely." She looped her arm through Niamh's.

Niamh took a moment to look at the girl beside her, deciding how best to bring Aodh into the conversation. Catrin, the younger of the queen's daughters, was a fifteen-year-old beauty with a big smile and even bigger dreams. Niamh knew the look in the girl's soft blue eyes. It was the same one she'd had until she realized her future had disappeared as suddenly as her monthly bleeding.

The worst part had been that when first it stopped, she'd naively believed that she carried Dallan's child. She waited for weeks, until she realized with horror that it was quite the opposite. In that moment, all her childish dreams had died alongside the realization that she would never carry Dallan's babe.

"I hope this isn't too intimate of a question," Niamh began tentatively, "but I couldn't help but notice you and your mother seem—distanced. I know a thing or two about mothers prying into your business, and, with your sister gone, I'd be happy to talk if you need a friend."

Catrin's young countenance hardened. "Well, it's all her fault, so it's hard *not* to be cross with her."

"How do you mean?"

"He was so kind, and *so* handsome. Such a skilled warrior, and a king himself, too! Then she had to go and ruin it."

"It sounds like you knew him well." Niamh had no idea how that might be possible, as according to Brona he appeared overnight and attacked at dawn. Aside from Cara's capture, it had sounded as though the family hadn't spoken with Aodh at all.

"Not as well as I'd have liked, of course. But the stories he told…" Catrin stopped abruptly, her eyes wide. "I mean, the stories others told about him. You know, it was as though I knew him myself."

"Of course," Niamh agreed politely. "Bards have such talent in bringing tales to life."

"Precisely."

It took all Niamh's presence of mind not to let her mouth drop open at Catrin's misspoken admission. Had Brona lied about Aodh's arrival? Had he come here prior to the attack? What on earth was going on? Niamh decided to press Catrin, in the hopes of getting some answers once and for all.

"Catrin, how exactly did your mother ruin everything?" Niamh ventured.

Catrin stopped walking and turned to face her. "You'll have to ask *her* about that," she whispered angrily. "And you should. Someone ought to know."

"But you can't tell me?"

Catrin resumed their circuit of the room, her voice still low. "It's not my secret to tell. And if she found out I had, she'd lock me away for the rest of my days."

Niamh didn't know if that was true or not, but she now knew one thing with absolute certainty: Brona had secrets.

And Niamh needed to uncover them.

CHAPTER SEVENTEEN

DALLAN HAD HIS work cut out for him. If Niamh insisted they had to start over, then that's exactly what he planned to do. He charmed her once, he could certainly do it again. And, though his mind told him he still risked having his heart broken a second time, Dallan found that the more time he spent around Niamh, the less he cared about that risk. Aye, it had begun as a truce to learn why she'd left. But now he found himself thinking as much of their future together as their past.

He remembered so many things about Niamh—the scent of lavender that followed her every step, the way her hair shone like gold and felt like silk in his hands, the sound she made when he—

"Are you ready?" The lady of his daydreams interrupted.

"Always." He winked at her playfully, rewarded by a deep, rosy blush on her cheeks.

He helped her mount her horse, letting his hands linger about her waist longer than necessary.

"I do believe you're trying to unsettle me," she proclaimed as they started down the path to Caiseal.

He grinned at her so that his dimples showed. "Is it working?"

"Not yet," she narrowed her eyes at him.

"Give it time."

Luckily for Dallan, time was something he currently possessed. Though the Fianna had made the ride from Caiseal in an hour's time to aid Thurles, Dallan had no intention of racing away his opportunity to talk with Niamh. Allowing their horses to walk at a leisurely, conversational pace, he had her all to himself until they reached Caiseal in several hours' time. They *could* make the journey in a day if they went straight to the market and back.

But they were absolutely staying overnight. Eva would never forgive him if they didn't.

Once they'd cleared Thurles and were well and truly on their way, Dallan dove in.

"Alright, tell me about yourself. I want to know *everything*."

Niamh giggled, looking at him in askance. "You're going to have to be more specific, I'm afraid."

"When did you become a healer? You never talked about healing at all, and now you've a reputation among the best."

Her face paled, and Dallan's heart sank. Why was he always getting it wrong? "I started studying herbs and treatments shortly after we left Nás." Her voice, barely audible over the soft breeze that swept over the forests and farms, warned Dallan he'd touched on a dangerous topic. "I fell into it rather by accident but, once I realized that I could help people, I kept going. It started with helping a neighbor with a cough, or a child with an upset belly. Then more and more folk started coming by, and I kept searching for better ways to help them."

"That doesn't surprise me at all," he replied sincerely. "If anyone needed help, you were always the first one there. And often the most capable, I might add."

"Flattery is unnecessary."

"It isn't flattery. 'Tis the truth. Do you think I would have trusted anyone else to help me hide Tóla's armor after he insulted my sister? Who else would have been brave enough to run through that bull's yard to save a duck?"

Her face lit up. "I forgot about the duck!"

Dallan hadn't. He remembered every moment of that year.

"Alright, so you like healing. You like ducks. You have a cat. What else? Do you still embroider?"

"You remember my embroidery lessons?"

Dallan swallowed. "I remember everything."

"Dallan—" she began.

But he didn't like the tone of her voice. He knew she was going to push him away again. So he stopped her.

"Now, hear me out. I know that, for whatever reason, six years ago you thought being with me was a terrible idea. But that was six years ago. We've both changed. You wanted to start over, to move forward. What if we did it together? Would it be so awful?"

"Why?" she asked. "Why do you still want me after everything that happened? Why waste your time falling in love with someone who could break your heart?"

That very thought had occurred to Dallan. Over the past few days, he'd slowly realized the answer. "Because I'm not falling in love with you. I've loved you for the past seven years, and I don't intend to stop anytime soon."

"I don't want to hurt you again." The pain in her voice nearly broke him.

"Then don't. Answer me one question, and we'll forget this whole conversation until you bring it up again." Dallan asked the question he hadn't been able to get out of his mind since the day of Aodh's attack. "Why are you wearing the ring?"

She looked down at the gold band, rolling it with her finger. "Because it feels like you're still with me when I have it."

Well, that cleared up nothing. And he'd sworn not to continue the conversation. So now instead of wondering why she wore the ring, Dallan was left to contemplate why she would leave him when she wanted him with her.

She seemed to sense his change of mood. "I know that probably doesn't make any sense to you," she admitted. "See, this is exactly what I meant. I'm still hurting you, even now, when I'm being honest."

"I don't know why you keep putting space between us." Dallan moved his horse closer, so that he could reach her hand. "I see in your eyes that you still care for me. I hear it in your voice, if not in your words. If you truly feel nothing, then tell me now and I will leave you be."

Dallan waited in the painful silence for her to deny any attraction between them. But the silence dragged on. After they crossed the River Suir, Dallan realized with relief that she wasn't going to push him away this time.

"I discovered something when I spoke with Catrin last night."

"Oh?"

"Catrin is fond of Aodh. Admiring, even."

"What? That makes no sense!"

"It gets better," Niamh continued. "She accidentally let slip that she's spent some length of time with him. She tried to cover it up, but it sounded as though Aodh was visiting in Thurles before the attack."

Dallan's mind raced to piece this new information into the story he'd already heard. "But Brona said Aodh's army appeared overnight," he thought aloud.

"Catrin said Brona had some sort of secret and we should talk to her to find out what really happened."

"I should speak with Brian while we're in Caiseal. He would want to know there's the potential for subterfuge."

"We also need to figure out how to get Brona to confess," Niamh added thoughtfully. "I doubt she'll simply offer up the information if we ask."

Dallan grinned at her, winning a smile in return.

"What?" she laughed. "Do you have an idea?"

"Do you know why we kept Diarmid behind?"

Her eyes went wide. "No!" She squeezed her eyes shut in a mixture of laughter and horror. "Tell me he isn't!"

"I don't think he's *actually* bedded her, but his entire job is to charm her into cooperating. She's taken a liking to him."

"But her husband just died!"

Dallan shrugged. "Not all marry for love. Perhaps they despised one another."

Niamh didn't appear to like that explanation but changed the subject yet again.

"So, tell me about the Fianna." He saw the eagerness, heard the curiosity in her voice. "I heard there were trials."

Dallan chuckled, squeezing her hand. "Is *that* ever a story. Lucky for you, we have some time."

THEY ARRIVED AT Caiseal far too soon for Dallan's liking. The sun sat high in the sky, lending what little warmth it could offer so late in the year. He'd only just finished answering all of Niamh's questions about the Fianna trials when their horses' hooves echoed through the courtyard.

Lorcán, the groom, looked at Dallan in concern as he took their horses into the stables. "Where are the others? Did they live?"

"Not to worry, Lorcán," Dallan assured him. "As far as I know, all are safe. I'm escorting this lovely lady on an errand. Do you know where my sister is?"

That calmed Lorcán, who directed Dallan to the hall. The groom disappeared with their mounts and handed their satchels to an errand boy.

Niamh fell into step behind him as they entered the hall. Eva, Dallan's sister, looked up as the doors to the hall opened. The moment she recognized them, she bolted from her chair in the most unladylike fashion that he'd seen from her yet.

"Dallan!" she squealed, rushing to embrace him. "Are you hurt?" She pulled back enough to check him over. "Where's Finn?"

"I'm fine. Finn's fine. He's out on another mission. We had a small errand to run in town here, and I couldn't pass by the opportunity to bother my baby sister."

"We?"

Niamh stepped out from behind Dallan, eliciting an ear-splitting yell from his surprised sister. She nearly knocked over Niamh as she pulled her into the world's tightest embrace.

"Niamh! I thought I'd never see you again! Lord, but you've

grown into a beauty. Come, we have so much to catch up on!"

Dallan couldn't help but wonder if they even remembered he stood beside them. "Uh, ladies," he called as Eva dragged Niamh deeper into the feasting hall. "What about the market?"

"You can go later," Eva replied. "You're staying the night, aren't you?"

"Yes, but—"

"We'll see you at supper, then! I'm sure Brian will find something to occupy you."

Grudgingly accepting his dismissal, Dallan watched his sister run into some hidey hole at the back of the hall with the woman he loved.

Maybe there was still some hope for them after all.

CHAPTER EIGHTEEN

NIAMH HARDLY MANAGED a backward glance at Dallan before Eva had her tucked away in an alcove. The keep at Caiseal felt gargantuan compared with Thurles. It even dwarfed Dallan's family seat at Nás. Set upon a hill, Caiseal stood tall and proud on the vast horizon, a cascade of farmland falling down its gentle slopes.

Eva had wound her way through a corridor at the back of the grand feasting hall, pulling Niamh behind her. They sat in a small alcove on a bench in front of the last window in the corridor. In the field below, men sparred with blunted practice swords. The clanging of their weapons and the shouts of frustration or exuberance easily masked any conversation the two women might have.

It had been six years since Niamh had last spoken with Eva, though they had always gotten on well. Eva had always been the opposite of her brother—soft-spoken and understated, though no less kind or clever for her reserve. Eva's pale brown hair fell to her back, the top half braided flawlessly. With deep green eyes and a fair complexion, Eva and her brother could hardly have looked less similar in appearance.

"I'll wager that Dallan will be on that field before we've finished talking," Eva declared. Her eyes might be a different color than her brother's, but they still sparkled with the same mischief.

Niamh couldn't argue with that. Dallan had always been a warrior. If he were forced to wait for the women to catch up,

Niamh didn't doubt for a moment he'd somehow end up with a sword in his hand.

"How long do you think it will take him to notice us?" Niamh asked.

Eva narrowed her eyes, taking in the field and men below. "I'm not certain he will," she ventured.

"So," Niamh began, "I believe congratulations are in order. Dallan tells me you've just gotten married."

A sweet blush ascended Eva's cheeks, followed by a smile. "Aye. I'm lucky to have found him. I couldn't have without Dallan, either. Did he tell you how it happened?"

Niamh watched Eva closely as she recounted her version of the tale Dallan had told on their way to Caiseal. Eva truly loved Finn. Niamh saw it in every word she spoke of him, in the tone of her voice, the tilt of her head, the faraway look in her eyes. Niamh had only met Finn once, briefly, before he'd been sent after the kidnapped princess. She would need to pay better attention next time, knowing he was married to such a dear old friend as Eva. She deserved only the best.

As Eva's tale came to a close, Dallan strode onto the practice field, taller and more handsome than any man in sight. He made all the other men look like young boys, at least as Niamh saw it. Dallan called the men around him, demonstrating several strokes with one of the practice swords before glancing briefly upwards.

Niamh's breath caught when his gaze fell on her, her heart racing as he smiled up at her.

"It seems I was mistaken," Eva admitted with a chuckle. "He noticed you right away."

For a brief moment, the world felt as it had six years earlier. Niamh sat with Eva, watching Dallan and talking of boys and marriage, placing wagers on how the men would do in their training. For one ephemeral glimmer, it all came back. Except it wasn't the same at all.

"I realize this is deeply personal, and we haven't spoken in years," Eva continued, her tone sobered, "but what happened?"

"It's hard to explain," Niamh hedged.

"I just," Eva sighed, "I thought everything was going so well with the two of you. And then I couldn't figure out why you never told me something was wrong."

Niamh heard the hurt, no matter how long past. She hadn't confided in her friend, and she hadn't even explained why they left. At the time all her thoughts had been on Dallan and her own troubles, but now she saw that he wasn't the only person she'd wounded.

She leaned forward, taking Eva's hands and squeezing them. "I am so sorry," she said quietly. "You're right. I should've spoken with you. You were one of my dearest friends, and I didn't think about your feelings at all."

"I was so worried about you," Eva replied. "I thought maybe Dallan had done something foolish and hurt you. I never thought him capable of such a thing, but I also never thought anything could go wrong for you two."

Niamh couldn't tell Eva why she'd left before Dallan knew. Something about it seemed wrong. But Eva deserved some manner of explanation.

"Dallan didn't do anything wrong," Niamh assured her. "He has always been the best man I know."

"Then why?" Eva's brows furrowed in concern.

"I can't tell you yet. Not before Dallan."

"You're going to tell him?" She sat straighter, wiggling closer. "Does that mean you're getting back together?"

"I don't know." Niamh admitted, falling back against the alcove's wooden wall. "I know he wants me to tell him why I left, and a part of me wants to, but I fear it will lead to a broken heart in time. And the only thing worse than losing him again would be to have him again and then lose him."

"This secret you're keeping, you think it will upset him? If it caused you to leave him, it cannot be a small thing. Is that your fear?"

"I don't think he'll be upset when I tell him." Niamh's heart sank at the notion. "I hope not. I think it will matter more to him later on, but he won't realize it until it's too late."

Eva nodded, her eyes pensive. "I think you should tell him. Not just the secret, but what you just told me—that you believe it will grow into a problem later."

"I'm worried at his optimism, his confidence. Normally those are things I love about him, but in this case I think it may serve his decision poorly. He'll wholeheartedly believe things will be alright—"

"And then they'll go sour," Eva finished. "Niamh, I want you to listen to me, as a friend. The biggest mistake you can make is to let fear keep you from love. Trust me, I know better than anyone. At least give it a chance. If you never take the risk, you'll never have an answer, and you'll spend your life wondering what it could have been."

"And," she added with a smirk, "if he breaks your heart I'll kill him. He knows better than to play havoc with my friend's heart."

CHAPTER NINETEEN

NIAMH WALKED BESIDE Dallan down the verdant hillside below the keep, reminding herself not to grab his hand every time it brushed hers. They decided to walk to the market, as neither one felt a particular need to ride again today.

After speaking with Eva, Niamh's resolve to stay away from Dallan weakened. Eva was right. Niamh's only chance at the life she truly wanted—a life with Dallan—began with a conversation she'd been avoiding for half a decade.

She felt more and more that telling him was the right decision. But to what end?

Would he take her back just like that, as though she hadn't broken his heart and disappeared for six years?

Would he treat her differently after he found out about her shortcoming?

Would he even still want her?

She'd never thought he would reject her outright when he discovered she couldn't conceive a child, but a lot can change in six years. Maybe he would lose interest in her over it. He certainly wouldn't be the first man to leave a woman over heirs.

The market square at Caiseal bustled with activity. Stalls and small shops surrounded a stone courtyard, children chased one another through the center, their laughter the only sound that rose above the murmur of haggling.

Niamh watched a rickety cart navigate the crowded thoroughfare, a pair of oxen plodding dutifully through the chaos.

Another, smaller cart sat alongside the road with a pack horse who looked less than pleased at her tethers.

"How do you train horses for battle?" Niamh wondered aloud.

Dallan followed her gaze to the cart and horses, standing beside her at the edge of the square. "The same way you learn to trust someone," he replied.

Niamh gave him a sharp look, not much caring for a platitude in place of an answer.

"Little by little," he grinned. "'Tis the same, really. If the horse doesn't trust you, no matter how used to the sounds and sights of a battle, you'll have trouble."

His fingers brushed hers for the hundredth time since they left the keep, sending yet another jolt through her, begging her for a response.

"You're doing that on purpose," she accused.

"Of course I am." This time he offered her his arm, nodding his head toward a nearby merchant stall.

Niamh considered not taking it. But, looking about at the press of people, she saw that it would be easier to stay beside him if she were attached to him. And she really wanted to touch him. Slowly, she settled her arm about his.

"You look as happy as Morrígan when she catches a fat mouse," Niamh teased, admiring the dimples that appeared on his cheeks. She'd always tried to get him to laugh just so she could see them. That was how she knew he smiled in earnest.

"Well, you always did have a way of making me laugh. Though you are both prettier and tastier than a fat mouse," he added.

"Truly, the highest praise I've ever received."

A strong, spicy scent filled the air about the merchant's stall, giving Niamh hope that perhaps she could find what she needed. As they waited for the bald, portly man to finish with another customer, Niamh perused the display of herbs and trinkets before her. In moments, she spotted the tiny, parchment-like scrolls of cinnamon bark.

"Do you have any oranges?" she asked the merchant when he finally turned his attention to them.

He narrowed his eyes, looking down his long, aquiline nose at her. "You aren't planning to eat them, right? Have you ever had one before?"

Niamh shook with irritation. *Of course* he would assume she knew nothing about them. She felt Dallan's arm tense beside her own.

Ignoring his questions, Niamh pressed on. "I need the peels, not the whole fruit."

"Well why didn't you say that to begin with?"

"Because oranges won't be in season for at least another month, and I assume it would be some time after that before you would get them here from so far south."

The merchant gave her an appraising look, then furrowed his considerable brows. "Those won't taste good either unless you have a plan for what to do with them. Sour as Satan, they are."

Niamh fisted her hands, suppressing a scream of frustration. It had been a long time since she'd had to buy from anyone other than the merchants who frequented Thurles.

"Are you going to sell her what she wants or not?" Dallan's low voice interrupted, irritated and possessive. It sent a tremor of heat coursing through her.

"I would love to, but I don't have any orange peels left. As she said, we're at the end of last season's stock for them."

Dallan looked about ready to jump over the wares and do battle with the bothersome man, so Niamh hurriedly spoke up. "I see you *do* have some cinnamon." She pointed at the aromatic sticks. "How much for them?"

"Six shillings a pound, they are. Or a third pound of silver, if you've no shillings."

Niamh's mouth fell open. "That's thievery!"

"They're a premium spice."

"I bought some a fortnight past for two shillings per pound, not a day's ride from here." Niamh didn't mention that the merchant she'd bought from was now buried next to the church in Thurles.

The merchant laughed—a sound Niamh could go her entire life without hearing again. "That man lost money."

"I'll pay three and no more." Even that was more than she'd wanted to spend, but the spice had a multitude of uses, not only for Alva but for many other conditions she treated.

"I won't sell for less than four."

Lord, but this man was trying her patience. "I have never, in ten years, seen them priced higher than three." Normally she would've walked away, but Alva was counting on her.

"Would you rather make three shillings or lose a sale?" Dallan interjected tersely.

Niamh worried the man wouldn't budge and they'd have come all this way for nothing. What would she do to keep helping Alva? She'd have to figure something else out.

After prolonged grumbling, he mumbled an agreement, taking her silver and weighing out her pound of cinnamon.

As they turned from the stall, Niamh beamed up at Dallan. "Thank you."

"My pleasure. I don't take kindly to merchants trying to swindle my friends," he growled. "Just ask Finn."

They made it to the beginning of the path up to the keep, a few steps from the market square, when Niamh stopped in the middle of the road.

"What's wrong?" Dallan asked, stopping beside a cloth merchant's shop and turning to face her.

Niamh looked first at the wooden walls of the shop, then at Dallan. She hadn't been able to stop thinking of her conversations with her mother and Eva. So much so that she was now considering just getting this over with so she could move on with her life.

"Why do you want to know why I left?" she asked.

A flurry of emotions passed over his face in rapid succession.

Confusion. Understanding. Irritation. Hope.

When he didn't answer, she offered more of an explanation. "What I mean is, to what end do you wish for this information?"

Still nothing. In fact, he appeared to not even be listening, though he was looking directly at her.

"Dallan?"

Recognition lit his face and he grimaced. "I'm so sorry. I thought I heard something. Could you say that again?"

"I asked why, after so long, you still want me to tell you why I left." She didn't try to hide her irritation that, of all their conversations, this was the one he couldn't be bothered to listen to. Perhaps this wasn't such a good idea after all.

"You want to know why I still—" his voice trailed off as his head turned back toward the market square, his jaw tight.

Was he angry with her? What a stupid question—of course he was! Deciding this, clearly, was not the right moment, Niamh gave up and began walking down the road toward the keep.

"Niamh!" Dallan shouted. "Wait, Niamh!" She heard the worry in his voice. "Behind you!" And ignored it.

He grabbed her arm, pulling her back to him so hard it likely left a bruise. The movement threw her off balance and straight into the wooden wall behind him.

Furious, she tried to escape, immediately stepping back toward the road.

He held her pinned against the wall, not budging in spite of her protest.

Seconds later, when she would have been a few steps on down the road, the cart she'd spied with the flustered pack horse came careening past. It flew by far too quickly to have stopped without hitting her, with no driver in sight. She stopped her protest as realization dawned.

He'd saved her life.

Cries from the market square told Niamh she hadn't been the only one in the cart's path. She and Dallan both turned to see a little boy of eight sitting beside his mother, who lay on the ground unmoving.

CHAPTER TWENTY

DALLAN COULD ONLY watch in awe as Niamh calmly kneeled beside the young boy and his mother. The woman's leg was obviously broken, given the way it laid, and her head was bleeding profusely. The boy sobbed loudly, watching Niamh work.

First, she checked the woman's head and eyes, then her neck and chest.

"Can you find linens?" she asked Dallan, not looking flustered or concerned in the least.

Dallan hurried to the cloth shop they'd passed, purchasing an armful of linen strips meant for just such a purpose. "What else do you need?" he asked, setting them down beside her on the stone courtyard.

"Honey for now. Then we should get her to the healer. I haven't any supplies to treat her properly."

"I've some at home!" a man called, running toward the nearest row of cottages.

A crowd had gathered around them, silent, their concern palpable.

"Is she alive?" the young boy ventured. "She's bleeding so badly."

Dallan went to sit behind the lad, watching Niamh work from the child's vantage point.

Niamh didn't pause, continuing to check the woman as she answered the boy. "She is. I believe she'll be just fine in a few weeks' time. Until then, though, she'll need your help."

"What can I do?"

"She won't be walking," Dallan explained, hoping to afford Niamh more concentration. "You'll have to carry things for her, help with meals, take care of the cottage. But she'll be better before you know it."

The boy sniffled, but his sobs subsided. "I think I can do that."

"You haven't a choice, lad," Dallan answered sternly. "If she has to move too much, she could get worse instead of better. Can I count on you?"

He nodded solemnly. "I promise. I'll take care of her."

"I know you will," Dallan assured him with a quick wink.

The man who'd left returned with two jars of honey, handing them to Niamh anxiously. She thanked him, setting them aside and handing the boy a strip of linen.

"Would you like to help?" she asked.

Dallan saw the fear in his eyes, but he nodded anyway. "What do you need us to do?" Dallan asked.

Relief washed over the boy's face when Dallan spoke. He picked up the linen, listening intently as Niamh explained how to hold it to the cut on his mother's forehead.

"It's not as bad as it looks there," she told him, her voice calm and confident. "When you cut your head it always bleeds a lot. Before we can bandage it, we need it to stop bleeding."

Dallan helped the boy apply pressure to the wound, both of them watching Niamh inspect the damaged leg. She looked back up at the lad. "Can you manage on your own a moment?"

When he nodded, she motioned Dallan over to her. "We need to set this before she comes to, otherwise it will be more painful for her."

Dallan had never seen this side of Niamh. Of course he'd seen her navigate difficult situations, or exercise skill in a task. He'd even seen her help a few of the survivors from the attack. But he'd never seen such an impressive combination of the two. For the first time since she'd fallen back into his life, he felt that he was really seeing her, seeing who she had grown into since they'd parted.

And she was incredible.

She talked him through helping her turn the leg so that she could use the honey to stave off ill humors and then wrap it tightly. "It'll need more work, but it's better done in the infirmary. This will suffice for now." She turned back to the lad. "How's the bleeding?"

He lifted the linen, showing that the flow had slowed significantly.

Niamh smiled at him. "You're doing wonderfully. Keep it there a bit longer, then we'll patch her up."

"Can she ride in a cart?" Dallan asked.

"A litter would be better if we can manage it. She shouldn't be shaken at all."

Dallan rose, asking around the crowd until he found someone with a large enough carrier. In no time, he and three men, along with the young boy, carried the woman to the healer's cottage on the edge of the village.

As it happened, Dallan knew the wise woman who healed folk in Caiseal. Maeve, a respected, bossy old crone with the kindest manner and the sharpest tongue. All the Fianna loved her dearly, a boon as they often had cause to visit her after battle.

When she heard the commotion, she opened the creaky door into her cottage and poked her head out.

"What's happened?" she asked Dallan.

"A cart hit her," he replied. "Niamh can tell you more."

"Lay her on the bed," Maeve instructed. She spotted Niamh behind the men, waving her over to the bedside. "What have you to tell me?"

As Niamh explained what they'd already done, Dallan helped settle the woman on the bed.

Then he moved to stand directly behind Niamh. Maeve glanced at him before returning her attention to Niamh. "Well, let's see how much damage you did, then."

Maeve assessed the woman, who was just beginning to wake. With an irritated grunt, she looked back to Niamh. "Seems you didn't do terribly."

"Of course I didn't," Niamh replied tersely.

Dallan suppressed a laugh at her boast—she sounded just like him.

"Where'd you find her, Dallan?" Maeve asked, nodding toward Niamh.

"Thurles."

That caught Maeve's attention. "Thurles, you say? You can't be the wisewoman I hear talk of—you're far too young."

Apparently Dallan wasn't the only one in awe of his golden-haired healer. "You've heard of her?" he asked with amusement.

Maeve folded her arms across her chest, regarding Niamh with open skepticism. "Aye. She's the best healer of women in the kingdom."

Dallan looked at Niamh. "Women, specifically?"

Niamh nodded but didn't offer an explanation.

"She has a reputation for helping women conceive children," Maeve continued. "And as a skilled midwife."

That must have been why Alva needed her help—to conceive a child. "Cinnamon?" Dallan asked.

Niamh nodded. "And oranges."

"And plenty of other things as well," Maeve interrupted. "Because I've tried those and it's never worked for me."

"I'd be happy to come here tomorrow before we leave and give you a list of my remedies," Niamh offered, "if there's a chance they will help someone."

If Dallan didn't know any better, he'd have sworn the old crone nearly smiled. Nearly.

"I'll expect you early. Don't keep me waiting. Now, you'd best go and let me get to work." She turned back to the woman on the bed, dismissing them.

Outside, the men had wandered back up the road with the boy. Dallan walked beside Niamh in companionable silence until they'd passed back through the village and were nearing the keep.

"I suppose I ought to thank you for saving my life," Niamh said softly, watching her feet as she walked.

"No thanks necessary," he replied. "If I let you get run down by a cart your mother would kill me. So, really, it was in my best interest to help."

She giggled and gave him a playful shove. "Thank you," she repeated, this time looking directly into his eyes.

"I believe," Dallan began tentatively, "that you were trying to tell me something important while I was distracted by the cart. I really do want to hear what you have to say."

"Perhaps another time," she replied softly, slipping her hand into his. "I've had enough excitement for one day."

CHAPTER TWENTY-ONE

HIS TIME WAS nearly up. Dallan entered the feasting hall at Caiseal consumed by worry over Morda's impending return. The day spent in Niamh's company had only deepened his desire to repair their past and build a future. It had also reminded him that he still had no guarantee of her returning such sentiments. Somehow, everything between them felt so easy, yet so hard all at once. Tonight, Dallan needed to determine her true feelings.

If she gave him even the slightest glimmer of hope, he would stay. He would make his home with Niamh, join Brian's family, stay with Eva and Finn and the rest of the Fianna.

If not, he would uphold his duty to family and return home to Laigin, where his people would have need of him in the coming years.

Dallan had attended several fine feasts in Caiseal since the Fianna arrived for their last trial, some weeks ago now. They had stayed on to help train Brian's army, and in that time several large banquets had come and gone, Eva and Finn's wedding his favorite. Though this dinner held none of the extravagance of past feasts, what it lacked in lavishness it made up for in charm.

As with most ancient halls, the large, central hearth burned like a beacon in the crowd, its bright, warm light a reassurance against Dallan's worries. Sparks flew up into the night sky through the smoke hole like stars returning home.

Eva sat down beside him, all smiles as she looked out at the merriment in the feasting hall. Dallan couldn't blame her—it was a joyful sight. Brian danced with Niamh, and Dallan found himself imagining a future where they were his family and Mumhain, his home.

"Could you imagine all of us returning to Cenn Cora together? Me and Finn, you and Niamh. How wonderful would that be?"

Dallan swallowed. It would be wonderful indeed, but right now it felt like a fool's hope.

"I may not be returning to Cenn Cora at all," he replied quietly. "Morda's recalled me to Laigin, but I haven't decided if I will go."

"Oh, Dallan." Eva shook her head sadly, placing a warm hand on his arm. "I do not envy you that decision. Have you told Niamh?"

"How could I? I can barely get her to speak to me sometimes. If I tell her I'm already thinking of leaving, she'd be gone from my life before I could say another word. I'm no fool, Eva," Dallan looked across the room at Niamh, dancing and smiling as though she hadn't a care in all the world. "I know that, for whatever reason, she doesn't trust me enough to tell me what's going on. I would destroy any progress I've made with her if I tell her about Morda."

"She wants to tell you," Eva whispered. "I'm not sure if it's you she doesn't trust, or herself."

Dallan's gaze shot to his sister. "She told you why she left?"

"No," Eva replied quickly, dampening his rising temper. "She didn't tell me why, just that she knew she needed to tell you eventually and she's worried over it."

"I would wait forever for her," Dallan admitted softly, "but I haven't the time. Morda will return any day now."

"I wish I could help you." Her sad smile didn't ease the growing ache in his chest.

"What would you do?"

"You know I would do anything for my family," she replied.

Dallan nodded in agreement, squeezing her into a small sideways hug. Aye, she'd more than proven it. After Morda and Sitric, their cousin, lost to Brian, Eva had volunteered as the hostage in the peace negotiations in order to spare the rest of the family from such a fate. She'd literally given up her future to secure everyone else's.

"But," she continued slowly, "now that I have Finn, I would always choose him."

Eva made a good point, but her situation was wildly different from Dallan's own. He knew that he would choose Niamh again, given the chance. The question was: would she choose him?

There was only one way to find out.

Though the next song had only just begun, Dallan wound his way through the hall until he reached his golden-haired beauty. "I'm afraid I can't bear to remain a bystander," he told Brian, though he captured Niamh's eyes, "and let you have all the fun."

"You're just in time, lad," Brian told him. "I was worried my wife would come looking for me. I thank you for the dances, dear."

"The pleasure was mine," she replied sweetly, taking Dallan's hand as Brian walked away.

"Do you remember the first time we danced?" Dallan ventured as they fell into step.

Niamh let slip a giggle before she suppressed her laughter. Lord, it felt good to see her smile. "How could I forget? It was your own fault for bringing the cat."

"If I recall correctly—and I always do—you refused to leave the wee beastie at the table. The *only* way I could convince you to dance was to bring her."

"She really did not like the bouncing," Niamh said, succumbing to laughter at the ridiculous memory.

Dallan's heart melted as he watched her. He felt as though he'd lived ten lives in the year they'd spent together. Every day had been an adventure.

"You didn't sneak her here without me knowing, did you?"

he teased.

"You know better than anyone she's impossible to keep hidden."

Though much of the lively dance was spent moving around one another, the few times they came together he savored the feel of his hands on her. It was impossible not to think about what he knew lay beneath her soft green gown, and how sorely he missed being the man she let in, the one she trusted.

As the song came to a close, he left his hand on her waist, waiting for her to push him away again, to put up another wall. Instead, she let her head fall onto his shoulder, walking tucked into his side back to the table for a drink.

"Niamh," he whispered into her golden hair, "I miss you."

She looked up at him, her pink lips drawing his immediate attention. "I miss you, too." Her smokey grey eyes told him she understood his meaning, that he wanted her back, wanted another chance. "But I need more time."

Dallan nodded, smiling softly and kissing the top of her head. If only he had time.

The sweet and spicy scent of lavender filled his lungs, and for the few moments it took to reach the table where Eva waited beaming at them, Dallan could almost imagine they'd never parted ways. He could almost convince himself that she hadn't really left him, that she loved him as deeply as he loved her.

Almost.

CHAPTER TWENTY-TWO

HER FIRST MORN back in Thurles, Niamh left her quarters just after the sun broke across the horizon, finally able to deliver an infusion of cinnamon bark to Alva after staying up late into the night to brew it. She'd also been able to restock the primrose oil and the tincture of raspberry leaves and milk thistle. She only lacked the bitter orange peel, but there was little she could do but wait a few months until they were in season. Hopefully it would be enough, for she didn't know how she'd carry on if she failed Alva.

She might not have been able to fix her own body, but she'd be damned if she didn't fix Alva's. Surely, they couldn't both be doomed to a life where they always felt lacking.

Before she'd even reached the courtyard, Brona approached her, looking even more determined than usual.

"Niamh!" she called, forcing Niamh to halt her own quest. "I was hoping to catch you."

Brona hurried over to her. "I'm just finishing up the planning for our grand Samhain Eve celebration. We've only two days left, and I'm assigning tasks to everyone in the keep."

Oh, lord. "What a lovely idea," Niamh replied cautiously. "I would help, but I'm afraid I'm still quite busy with the—"

"Nonsense." Brona's tone left no room for further disagreement. "I want everyone to feel that they are a part of the celebration. I'm placing you in charge of hanging boughs in the feasting hall. They'll need to be up by midday on Samhain Eve."

Irritation flared, but Niamh kept it to herself. She had more than enough to do, and the last thing she needed was one more task. Especially for a celebration that no one really wanted right now. Sensing defeat and swallowing her objections, Niamh shifted her focus back to the most important task: checking on Alva.

"They will be." Niamh didn't try to hide her lack of enthusiasm for the project. "Have you happened to see Alva about yet this morn?"

Brona pursed her lips thoughtfully. "I might have seen her near the infirmary."

Niamh thanked her and hurried toward the infirmary. Alva had probably been there to ask after the infusion. Grumbling at the delay, and the possibility she'd already missed her, Niamh threw open the door to the small outbuilding where she spent most of her days.

To find Dallan waiting for her.

Mumbling an exasperated oath, she contemplated simply turning back around to find Alva. Niamh didn't want her to go any longer than necessary without her treatments, and it had already been far too long. But Dallan spotted her the moment she stepped inside, his face creasing in concern at her poor greeting.

"Let me guess," he declared, his tone playful. "You've missed me so much since we parted yesterday afternoon that you knew, the moment you saw me, you wouldn't be able to resist my incredible charm. Is that about right?"

Niamh smiled, shaking her head. "It *is* incredibly difficult, but somehow I'll manage." It was impossible to be upset when Dallan was with her. If he turned on his charms, it felt as though the sun were shining directly on her, warm and welcoming and pushing her to shine right alongside it.

He sat atop her work table, patting the smooth surface next to him.

Niamh complied, feeling pulled in a hundred directions.

Just as she did every time she saw him.

She wanted to be his again. She missed him.

She loved him.

And she knew she had to tell him soon. She had already waited too long. What if he got tired of waiting on her? But even if he accepted her now, there was no guarantee of forever, no promise of future happiness to be had.

Dallan helped her up onto the table beside him, turning her insides into an explosion of butterflies. Just as he always had.

"Are you still angry with me?" he asked, the concern on his face heartbreaking.

"What?" Niamh answered a little too loudly. "No, I was never angry with you. It's Brona and the ridiculous decorations. And I've been trying to find Alva but instead I keep finding everyone else. Or, rather, everyone else keeps finding me."

"Decorations?"

"Yes, decorations," Niamh huffed. "As if I need yet another thing to worry over. And everyone knows she's just making a pathetic attempt to distract everyone from all the danger we're actually in. It's like she refuses to face the reality of her situation. And, on top of all of it, how in the world am I supposed to hang anything in the hall? I can't even reach the rafters!"

Dallan fought the smile threatening his lips, clearly amused by her outburst. "I could help."

"That's very kind, but I'll manage. Perhaps I can find a ladder."

"That won't help in the middle of the hall," he pointed out, hopping off the table and reaching to his full height—tall enough to nearly touch the beams of the infirmary. "See," he grinned wickedly. "You need me."

"Absolutely not." She crossed her arms. "Why are you here, anyway? Did you need something?" They hadn't made any sort of arrangement to meet again after returning from Caiseal. In fact, they'd hardly talked at all the entire ride back to Thurles.

He'd asked if she was still angry with him. Was that why he'd been so quiet? What would she even be angry about?

Dallan stood an arm's length from where she still sat upon the table. He ran his tongue over his teeth—in a manner Niamh found truly distracting—before finally answering her question.

"I wanted to see if you were able to get Alva sorted after all the trouble you went to over the cinnamon." He looked down at his feet halfway through his explanation.

"You're a terrible liar," Niamh teased. "You always look at your feet."

"And you always catch me." This time he looked her directly in the eyes. "I feel that we left things unsaid after the journey. I don't want to keep it that way."

Niamh swallowed. She meant to tell him, but not like this. She needed time to choose her words more carefully, to prepare herself.

"What things?" she asked.

"I'm sorry that I upset you," he replied quietly. "I hope I didn't hurt you too badly when I pulled you off the road. I should've been paying more attention."

"No," Niamh breathed in relief. "You should never apologize for saving someone's life. You didn't upset me at all. Forget the whole thing."

He stepped toward her, now within easy reach. "You're certain?"

Niamh grabbed a small bag off the table beside her, handing it to Dallan. He took it, opening it and smelling the contents.

"Cinnamon?"

"I set some aside for you while I made up Alva's infusion. As a thank you."

He said nothing, staring at the bag.

"It's not much," Niamh continued, now wishing she'd done more. "If you'd like I can make you that drink you like so much, with milk and cinnamon. Dallan?"

"You remembered," he sounded so far away. "You remembered that it was my favorite."

Niamh's heart melted into a puddle in the pit of her stomach.

He looked so vulnerable, so much like that boy she'd fallen in love with.

"Of course, I remembered. You didn't honestly think I could buy cinnamon and not set some aside for you? You had my father on contract to let you know the moment he restocked it." She smiled at the memory.

He swallowed hard, taking a shaky breath. "I haven't had it in ages. Your father thought it the most ridiculous request," he laughed.

"Aye, but he'd have done anything for you. And we all knew how seriously you took your cinnamon."

"There's nothing else like it," he defended. Then his face fell. "Your father—what happened to him?"

"He's gone." That was Niamh's answer anytime someone asked after him. He'd abandoned her mother once it had become clear she'd not be giving him any more children and Niamh wouldn't be marrying a prince. As far as Niamh was concerned, he was as good as dead anyway, so it wasn't entirely untrue.

"I'm so sorry, Niamh," Dallan took another step closer. "I can't imagine how hard that must have been on you and your mother."

The door opened to the infirmary and Alva stepped inside. Niamh exhaled in relief.

"Am I interrupting?" she asked.

"Not at all," Niamh replied. "I've been hoping to find you this morning. Come on in."

Dallan stepped back, leaving Niamh wishing they had more time to speak. Alva moved out of his path through the doorway, walking over to Niamh expectantly. Before Dallan shut the door, he turned back to Niamh.

"I'll see you Samhain Eve."

"Dallan," she started in protest.

"We hang the boughs at the third bell," he interrupted with a wicked grin. He turned and left, with his cinnamon in one hand and her heart in the other.

She looked at Alva, who covered her mouth to suppress a giggle.

"I am in so much trouble."

CHAPTER TWENTY-THREE

D ALLAN HAD KNOWN this day would come, and yet it didn't make the decision any easier. When Cormac summoned him to the solar the next afternoon with a message that he had a guest, Dallan knew he could no longer avoid making his choice. Would he return to his family? Or would he keep waiting on Niamh? Did it need to be one or the other?

The weather had begun to turn, the rain colder and more frequent as winter teased at the edges of autumn. It should be weeks before the cold came in full, yet as Dallan crossed the courtyard in Thurles, it wouldn't have surprised him if it began to snow. Though he had turned the decision over and over in his mind, he remained undecided. Dallan knew that he should be motivated by ties to family and political maneuvering. Or, at the very least, by what he felt most compelled to do with his life. Yet for some reason, Dallan found the only thing that mattered to him, the thing to which he always returned, was his relationship with Niamh.

It hadn't taken long after seeing her again for Dallan to realize that, in spite of their past, he still wanted her in his life. The question was: Did she want him in hers?

And *that*, for Dallan, would be the deciding factor. If Niamh weren't in the picture, he knew he would return to Laigin and help his uncle. As Brian had said, family was everything.

But if he could start his own family with Niamh, he would stay in Brian's service. He knew she had no great desire to be a queen, as they'd discussed it many times when they first courted. For years Dallan thought she'd left because of it, at least in part. But now that he'd finally spoken with her, his gut told him there was more to it than that.

As he neared the solar, Dallan wished he had more time. He needed longer to get Niamh to trust him, to open up to him so that he could finally fix whatever had gone wrong. Opening the door, Morda stood to greet him once again.

"I went to Caiseal," his uncle said with a chuckle, "not realizing you'd been called away to Thurles."

"You saw Brian?"

Morda nodded. "He kindly pointed me in the right direction."

"I'm not ready." Dallan saw no reason to dance around the matter. "I need more time."

"I'm sorry, lad. I wish I could give it to you, but we're both needed back in Laigin. I can't linger here much longer, and I must know your answer before I go."

Dallan couldn't sit. Instead, he paced before the hearth, pulse racing as he prayed for time.

"What's got you so unsettled?"

Dallan hesitated. "Niamh."

"What?" Morda's heavy brows furrowed. "The woman who left you years ago?"

"She lives here," Dallan sighed, finally collapsing into a chair. "She's the healer."

"I see." Morda sank into the chair opposite him, looking for all the world like Dallan's father when he was about to give a talking-to. "She can come with you, lad. Bring her back to Laigin."

He shook his head, looking down at his folded hands. "I don't know if she would go."

"Tell it to me straight," Morda demanded gently. "What's going on with her?"

"That's just the trouble. I don't know." Dallan stood again, running a hand through his tangle of dark waves. "Once we got past the initial awkwardness, it felt as though we'd never been apart. But she still won't tell me why she left. And even though we've been getting on well enough, she keeps me at arm's length, pushing me away at every turn."

He risked a look at Morda's expression and regretted it immediately. He wasn't looking for pity. Gritting his teeth, he returned to pacing.

"Has she given you any indication that she's even interested?"

"I gave her an opportunity to be rid of me for good and she didn't take it," Dallan admitted, realizing how bad it sounded when he spoke the words aloud.

"Let me be clear," Morda replied sternly. "I am one of the most biased people to get advice from on the matter, as I want nothing more than for you to accompany me back to Laigin tonight. That being said, if she won't talk about your past, won't agree to a future, pushes you away, and is altogether noncommittal, it seems to me she's just not interested, lad."

"Well, when you say it like *that*," Dallan grumbled. He hated to admit it, but it did indeed sound that way.

"If Niamh weren't here, what would you do?"

"I would go with you."

"Don't wait around to have your heart broken a second time. You and I can travel the nine kingdoms together until we find a woman for you."

Dallan couldn't put voice to how much he disliked that idea. Instead, he simply shook his head.

"Give it time," Morda assured him. "I propose that you swear your vow to me tonight, take your place as second. Take two days to farewell your friends and convince your lady, then meet me at Nás after Samhain."

Dallan nodded, still shaken by the realization that perhaps Niamh truly wanted nothing to do with him. If she did, wouldn't she have said as much by now?

"I'm understanding, lad, but I've also got a kingdom to mind. And," Morda hesitated, "I may not have been as clear on my reasons for insisting on your return."

Dallan didn't like the look that crossed his uncle's face. In all his life, all the decades that Morda had been king, Dallan had never seen a look such as the one he saw now. A look of fear.

"What's going on?" he asked, hoping he misread his uncle's expression.

Morda shifted in his chair. "Fachtna has not handled Baeth's death well."

"Something tells me that's an understatement." Fachtna, another of Dallan's uncles, had always had designs upon Morda's throne. In recent years, he'd begun attempting more openly to convince the small council—the group of lesser kings who advised Morda—that he would be a stronger leader. His son, Baeth, had supported his efforts—until his death in battle against Dallan. When Dallan had left Laigin, Fachtna had managed to stir the pot, but Morda's decades-long reign had held fast. "What has he done?"

"Well, after losing at Dyflin and being forced to support Brian in his bid for the high kingship, it seems some of the council members are more open to considering Fachtna's claim to the throne."

"He's going to try to kill you," Dallan warned. "If the loss is enough to gain support, it won't be long before he and the others take the throne by force."

Morda leaned forward onto his elbows. "Which is why I need one of the best warriors in the nine kingdoms by my side. I admit, my position is weakening by the day and I cannot guarantee your safety. But I would ask your help."

Dallan sighed. No matter how he felt about Niamh, or the Fianna, or his new life here, he could not sit idly by and watch his kingdom crumble. "I'll do it."

"I know it's a great sacrifice and a great risk," Morda replied. "Thank you. I will do everything I can to keep us both alive, but in the end the kingdom is what matters. We must maintain the peace."

"Entirely fair," Dallan agreed. He'd spent the last year helping Eva get settled into her new life. Now, it was time for him to help the rest of the family.

As he spoke the words to his uncle that had been passed down for countless generations of kings, Dallan couldn't stop thinking about Niamh. And Finn. And Diarmid and Cormac and Conan. Even Brian. All the new friends he'd only just made that he would now be leaving. But family was everything, and Dallan's family needed him.

CHAPTER TWENTY-FOUR

Samhain Eve came entirely too quickly for Dallan. Cormac kept him busy for the rest of the day after Morda's visit, taking away any hope Dallan had of stealing another meeting with Niamh. He'd thought of her nearly every moment since she'd handed him a bag of cinnamon.

He needed to speak with her about returning with him to Laigin. Though, after hearing more of the details and learning just how dangerous the politics had become, he wasn't entirely certain he wanted her there just yet. By the end of that day, however, Dallan knew he couldn't make that decision for her. He would tell her everything and let her decide.

Since she'd come back into his life, Dallan had wavered in his resolve to continue seeking her out. At first, he'd wanted nothing to do with her. But once they'd gotten past the initial shock of their chance meeting, he started remembering all the reasons he'd fallen in love with her in the first place. And he could see in her eyes that she still enjoyed his company, still felt as drawn to him as he did to her.

Moment by moment, they'd built a tentative, new friendship.

Except the more time he spent with her, the more he realized he didn't want only her friendship. He still wanted *her*.

But she was not the carefree girl he'd courted. She was a woman full-grown who held painful secrets beneath her somber expression. And he knew he'd never have all of her until he uncovered the truth of it. So, the question became, was the risk worth the reward?

The moment she handed him the cinnamon, he realized the answer had always been "yes."

He strode into the hall, a mug of warm milk with cinnamon and honey in each hand and a grin on his face. He needed his charm at full force if he was somehow going to convince her to go to Laigin with him after Samhain. He knew she'd give him trouble for pushing his help on her, but he also had no intention of letting her do anything so foolish as to try to balance a ladder unassisted in the middle of the hall.

Which was exactly what she was doing when he spotted her.

"Where is everyone?" he asked, walking over to her ladder and taking in the oddly quiet hall. Normally *someone* was inside, either for the warmth, companionship, food, or rest. Or to see to a duty. But there was no one, not even the servants.

"Brona sent them off. She wanted them to be surprised."

"By your swift and violent demise?"

"I'm doing just fine," she called, reaching precariously to hang a strand of oak-leaf garland on a hook in the rafters.

He set the mugs down on the nearest table, leveling her with a skeptical stare. "You are wobbling atop a ladder, supported only by a table that is far too small. You're lucky I got here before you broke your neck."

"I'm not going to break my neck."

"Aren't you the healer?" He watched her closely as they spoke, knowing it was only a matter of time before the ladder gave way. "Who do you think will heal you when you're grievously injured?"

She stopped working long enough to glare at him, her gaze falling from him to the mugs of spiced milk.

"I brought you a drink," he explained. "A token of good intention, if you will."

Her face softened, a smile playing at the corner of her lips. "Warm milk and cinnamon?"

"With honey, of course," he scoffed mockingly. "I'm not an

animal."

She giggled, at the same time reaching for the next hook. The ladder slipped from the table's edge. And Niamh fell straight into his waiting arms.

"I've got you," he assured her, his heart hammering in his chest.

She stared at him, her grey eyes wide in shock. "I can't believe that just happened." Her voice was the faintest whisper, filled with disbelief.

Dallan should have helped her back to her feet. He should have made a joke about how he was always right. He should have handed her a mug of cinnamon milk to calm her nerves.

He definitely should not have kissed her.

But something about holding her in his arms, alone in the dimly lit hall, destroyed what little restraint he had left. Her parted lips called to something primal, something he'd buried deep within, but now that it had escaped, he was helpless to stop it.

His lips brushed hers softly, questioningly. And she answered.

Her hands pulled at his shoulders, her chest now pressed tightly against his own.

He couldn't take any more torture—he needed his hands back. Dallan turned, setting her on the table in front of him. He didn't dare risk taking his lips from hers, so he moved slowly, his hands pulling her hips against him.

Every memory of every time he'd held her in his arms filled each breath they shared. Now that he had her back there, he knew he couldn't live without her again.

His hands ran along her body, soaking in the warmth of her delicious curves. He captured her moan in his kiss.

Niamh's soft lips parted, her tongue demanding more.

And Dallan gave it to her. He gave her the kiss he would've given her if she'd accepted his proposal that night. The one that told her how much he wanted her, how much he needed her.

How much he loved her.

He never expected she'd kiss him back with the same urgency.

When she pulled away from him, he cupped her cheek with his hand, rubbing her smooth skin gently.

"Dallan."

The pain in her voice when she said his name would've broken his heart all over again—if there hadn't also been passion laced through it. At least he knew she returned some of his feelings, if not all.

"What do you want from me?" she asked.

A thousand responses played through his mind because, in truth, he wanted it all. A courtship, a marriage, a family, a future. Her laugh, her wit, her companionship. But he also wanted an answer that wouldn't destroy this hard-won moment.

"I want another chance."

"You don't need one," she whispered. "I'm the one who ruined it."

Dallan's pulse raced. Was she finally going to open up to him? Terrified he'd say something wrong, he said nothing at all.

"I will tell you everything tonight," she promised, worrying her lip. "But I think I should answer at least one of your questions."

"Niamh, we don't have to talk about anything now," he hurried. "Let's just start over."

She shook her head. "We can't. I'll explain, but it just—it won't be that easy."

He didn't know what to make of such a statement. What could be so wrong, that he hadn't done, that still needed to be addressed six years later?

"I wear the ring because I never stopped loving you," she said. "And it reminds me that there was a time when you loved me, too."

Dallan felt the world tilt beneath him. Somehow more comforted and more confused all at once, he told her the only thing he could think of—the truth.

"Niamh, I never stopped loving you, either. Now that I've spent time with you again, I know that it was no accident that brought us together, no coincidence. We are meant for one another, and I will wait as long as I must for you to see it."

Her eyes fell back to his lips. "How about we start with just another kiss?"

"Now that," Dallan said, closing the distance between them, "is your best plan yet."

CHAPTER TWENTY-FIVE

A T SUNSET THAT same day, Niamh entered the hall beside her mother and Máire, her nerves so taut they could shoot an arrow. She and Dallan had somehow managed to get the hall decorated before Brona came to inspect near midday, and the fruits of their hard work hung from the rafters and walls. The hall sparkled like a forest at midnight, candles in braziers flooded the shadowy room with orange light beneath a canopy of verdant boughs. Jugs of wildflowers, roses, and oak leaves sat atop each table.

"What if I'm making a huge mistake?" she whispered frantically.

"He's not your father," her mother replied under her breath. "At least give him a chance."

Looking about the room, she spotted Dallan speaking with Cormac and Diarmid near the hearth at the center. As soon as he saw her, a dashing smile broke across his handsome face and he started toward her.

Niamh braced herself. She felt as though she were falling from a cliff, knowing she'd crash into an unpredictable sea. But the only way forward was to swim. Her mother gave her hand a supportive squeeze before disappearing into the crowd with Máire.

Every time Niamh saw Dallan, her heart leaped at the same moment as guilt swept through her for continuing to keep her secret from him. Whether she thought it a terrible idea or not, she and Dallan were building a new relationship. She couldn't let the secret that had destroyed the old become the foundation of the new. Of all the people in her life, he deserved the truth most of all. And tonight, she would see that he got it. And a little adventure besides.

"You look ravishing this evening," he drawled, eyeing her from head to toe. "I do believe blue is your color."

She took the arm he offered. "You're a shameless charmer," she teased.

"Guilty." His chestnut eyes sparkled with mischief as he led her toward the center of the hall.

Niamh tugged him the other direction, toward the door out to the courtyard. "And far too handsome for your own good."

"Still guilty."

She didn't even try to suppress a giggle at his boast. She had always loved his confidence. As they stepped from the warm hall into the chilly autumn air, Dallan pulled her to a stop.

"I can't help but feel that you're up to something," he said, shooting her the most adorable, accusing look.

"Do you remember the ghost flower?"

His mouth opened first in shock, then in mischief. "You're serious?"

"Oh, come on," she pleaded. "How long has it been since we've gone on an adventure together?"

"Every time I go on an adventure with you, I end up either saving your life or defending mine from my livid parents. Often both."

Niamh fell immediately into the role she'd adored but long since abandoned—the instigator. Luckily for her, Dallan never turned down an adventure. And he *never* backed away from a challenge.

Placing her hands on her hips, she stared him down with all the intensity she could muster. "You're just afraid of the ghosts, aren't you?"

"I see," he narrowed his eyes at her. "So that's how it's going to be, is it?"

"Look, if you're too scared all you have to do is tell me."

"I know what you're doing, you know. We've had this conversation a hundred times."

"And?"

He threw his head back, highlighting his strong jaw and wide chest. "God help me, it's working. Is that bad?"

"Terrible," she laughed, yanking on his arm again. "Let's go."

She led Dallan to the stables, watching him ready his horse with practiced efficiency. He had grown far more serious in the years they'd been apart. This seemed to her the best way to finally open up to him, to offer to start again—sharing another adventure. It had never felt right to go on one without him, so it had been years since Niamh had done anything this spontaneous.

"Alright," he said, setting the reins in place and helping her onto the horse behind him. "Where to? Tlachtga and Tara are too far for one night's ride."

"The Caiseal."

He turned to look at her, his brows knitted. "Caiseal's too far as well."

"Not Caiseal, *the* Caiseal," she replied. "You know, Cnoc Rua, The Red Hill."

"Cnoc Rua? That place is haunted."

"Aye. By ghost flowers."

He turned around with her favorite put-upon sigh—something she'd missed more than she'd expected—and nudged the horse across the courtyard to the gate. "You're going to be the death of me, Woman." Even as he said the words, she could hear the smile in his voice.

"I CANNOT BELIEVE you talked me into this," Dallan whispered, pulling his cloak tighter as they stood at the foot of Cnoc Rua.

A gently sloping hill flowed like a skirt of green from a circle of giant standing stones. The charcoal sky surrounded them, the moon shining silvery light onto the ancient tomb. Long ago, an earthen mound had been built inside the stones, but only a handspan here and there remained around the circle. Niamh couldn't even imagine how long ago it was built to have eroded so much already.

"We always said we'd go," Niamh whispered back. It felt inappropriate to raise her voice, so she matched his hushed tone.

A breeze rushed by, whistling over the rocky hillside and chilling Niamh to the bone. She shivered beneath her own cloak but pressed onwards. "It'll be fun," she added hesitantly.

Taking a deep breath, she took several steps up the gentle hill when a warm weight enveloped her shoulders, startling her.

Dallan's deep, low voice spoke closer than she'd expected, sending chills of anticipation down her spine. "You're shivering."

So he'd given her his cloak, ever the honorable prince.

"Won't you be cold?"

His hand brushed a stray strand of hair from her cheek. "I'll be fine."

As he looked into her eyes, his jaw tightened, like he was swallowing down his desire. Niamh's stomach flipped when she realized that was likely exactly what he was doing.

Remembering their kiss earlier that day, her eyes fell to his lips, willing him to kiss her. Instead, he took a step away.

"So what does this ghost flower look like?" he asked, taking her hand and leading her to the top of the hill.

Now that they were closer, the stones felt like a third person joining them for the evening. Some were large—as tall as Dallan. Others only reached Niamh's ankle.

"It's white, I should think."

He leveled her a look. "You don't *know* what it looks like?"

"I'll know it when I see it."

He shook his head with a sideways grin, looking intently at the ground as he started wandering the clearing.

Niamh went the opposite way, running her hand along the cool stones as she walked. They had designs carved into them, swirls and lines and all manner of patterns. Invisible in the dark, only the tips of her fingers knew of the secret spirals that followed her around the mound. She came upon a group of the tallest stones, stacked together to form a small corridor. As she rounded the outside corner of the structure, Dallan jumped out from the other side, scaring her silly.

Her scream echoed off the stones, followed by his laughter.

"I'm sorry," he managed, bending over as he laughed at his joke. "I couldn't resist."

She couldn't believe she'd spent years away from him. Dallan had been her best friend since that day in the courtyard seven years ago. Living without his ridiculous jests and endearing boasts, his quiet courage and unwavering support—living without *him*—Niamh realized she hadn't really been living at all.

"I need to tell you something, and I want you to know that this is quite difficult for me, so please be patient if I don't explain it terribly well."

Dallan took her hands in his, warm and strong. "There's something I want to tell you as well. You go first, though."

"When we left Nás," she began, "it wasn't only because I'd refused your betrothal. When I told you my father was gone, I didn't mean he'd died. He left us. His family found him another wife, and he left us to go marry her."

Dallan looked so horrified that it gave Niamh hope. "What?" he exclaimed, clearly shocked. "Why would he do such a thing?"

Niamh's heart pounded so loudly she could hear it in her ears. Summoning all the courage she had, she looked him dead in the eyes. "My mother couldn't have any more children. One daughter was not enough."

He squeezed her hands, understanding flooding his handsome face. "And it is a common condition in your family?"

Niamh swallowed, lightheadedness descending. "I knew for certain I had inherited the same condition a few weeks before he left. My bleeding had stopped long before, but that wasn't too alarming. It had come and gone for years. A small part of me had even dared to hope that I carried your child.

"But then I started having the bursts of hot and cold that my mother had. Her sister had the same symptoms when she was young, but my mother's didn't develop until later. I should have left with him, instead of waiting for you to propose. I shouldn't have waited so long. It was cruel to do it when I did, and I'm so sorry. I didn't know what else to do."

She watched his mind consider all that she'd just shared. "You accidentally became an expert in women's care because you were searching for ways to heal yourself."

"I found so many ways to help women conceive, and carry healthy babies, and even recover afterward." Tears gathered in the corners of her eyes. "But I couldn't find any way to heal myself."

"Niamh," his soft, smooth voice washed over her like cool water on a balmy day. "I love *you*. I love you whether we have children or not. As long as I have you, nothing else matters."

The tears escaped, one by one, salty streams carving paths down her cheeks. "But you're a prince," she explained. "Your family will expect you to have heirs."

"If that's enough for my family to disapprove of you, the devil can take them for all I care."

"Really?"

"Yes." Dallan's firm answer finally gave her the solid ground she'd been searching for since they'd met again. "Is that why you left? Because you feared their disapproval?"

"I—" she paused, hardly able to form the words that had haunted her for so long. "I feared you might one day leave. Maybe not right away, but once you realized the truth in it. When we'd struggled for years with naught but frustration and grief."

"You thought I would leave like your father did, abandon you when you were hurting, when you needed someone most." He let out a shaky breath. "Niamh, look at me."

She raised her gaze, unable to hold in the flood of tears now.

"We will not have years of struggling to have children. We

will have years of love and joy in each other. We will have years of warm milk with cinnamon, laughing so hard we can't breathe, and taking care of that damned cat. And you have my vow that should I ever be so lucky as to have you as my wife, I will never, ever leave you."

She didn't deserve him. He was always so kind, so sweet and thoughtful. She would spend her entire life trying to become the kind of woman who was worthy of such a man.

"I love you, Dallan," she replied, throwing herself into his arms and holding him tight.

"I love you, too." He smiled down at her, their noses touching as they both laughed. "So would you like to court again, or skip back to the proposal?"

"Are you asking me to marry you?"

"Only if you'll agree this time," he teased.

Niamh's heart soared. She had expected him to be understanding and even accepting. She hadn't expected him to not care at all. It felt so good to finally tell him, to no longer carry the weight of her secret.

"I'm already wearing the ring, aren't I?"

"Fair point." He took her hand, toying with the gold band on her middle finger. "How badly do you want this ghost flower?"

"Why?"

"Because there's something I'd like quite a bit more." The hungry look in his eyes brought the butterflies back to her stomach with a vengeance.

CHAPTER TWENTY-SIX

I N RESPONSE TO his bold suggestion, Niamh leaned toward him, her lips parted temptingly.

He didn't think. He reacted. Pulling her into his arms, he met her with a searing kiss, the kind he had dreamed of every night since she left. Hot and hungry and filled with six years of waiting for this moment, of being tortured by memories of all the other times he'd held her like this.

Her hands wound through his hair as the wind whipped over the ancient hilltop. She matched his enthusiasm, igniting a fire deep in his belly.

Every muscle in his chest tensed—he felt invincible, like he could take on anything. Gently, he backed her against one of the tall stones. Her sharp intake of breath as he loosened her gown drove him mad with desire. He wanted to spend the night worshipping every inch of her.

His hands greedily roamed her glorious body. He began at the generous curve of her hips, following the feminine lines of her up her slim waist and back out again where her breasts tested the lacing of her gown. She arched into his touch as he strayed to cup her breasts, teasing him through the thick fabric. Dallan lost all ability to reason. His fingers played at her collar, his lips tasted the sensitive skin down her neck. He wanted to devour her.

The wicked wind set her hair dancing, surrounding him in a golden veil that smelled of lavender and Niamh. She ran her hands under his *léine*, a shiver of pleasure following in their wake.

With a playful squeeze to her backside, he lifted her up, keeping one hand beneath her to support her against the stone. Niamh's giggle of surprise rang like a chime across the hilltop.

"I don't think we've tried it this way before," she said breathlessly, reaching between them to free him from his trews.

He didn't know how he'd gone so long without her. "I'm stronger than I was then," he managed as she took him in hand. Dallan tossed her skirts out of the way.

Her hooded eyes drank in his shoulders and arms. It had been so long since anyone had looked at him that way, since he'd let anyone see that side of him.

Since he'd let himself be so vulnerable.

He'd never admit it to any of the Fianna, but when Niamh left she'd taken a part of him with her. And even years later, he'd never been able to give that part to anyone else. Oh, he'd tried to bed other women, desperate to take his mind off the only woman he really wanted. But only Niamh coaxed out this teasing, playful, wild side of him. A side that, until this moment, he hadn't realized how much he'd missed.

His fingers played with her, eliciting a moan as she moved against him. He slipped one inside, but it wasn't enough. Dallan didn't know how long it had been since she'd been with someone, and he didn't want to rush her, so he sucked in a breath and circled her with his thumb.

"Please," she whispered. "Stop teasing." She didn't wait for his response, quite literally taking matters into her own hands. Lifting her hips, she seated herself on top of him with a little noise that nearly undid him.

He thrust himself inside her again, wondering how long he'd be able to endure such sweet torture. She protested when he stopped a moment later. But he had a very good reason for halting. As quickly as he could manage, Dallan reached up to finish loosening her gown, tugging it until her full breasts sat naked before him.

"That's better," he growled, leaning to take one of her pert nipples into his hungry mouth. Then the world dissolved around him. It was only Dallan and Niamh. Her scent, her sounds, her hands, her warmth—they were his entire existence.

Dallan had no idea how long he made love to her on the stone-strewn hilltop beneath a dusting of stars in the midnight sky. Niamh cried out his name, tightened around him, sending a surge of desire through him. He held her against his chest as he found his release just after hers.

Dallan struggled to slow his breathing as he rested his forehead against hers. He could feel her heart racing, hammering in a rhythm to match his own. He could hardly believe that he had Niamh back. After talking with Finn, he had hoped to perhaps earn enough of her trust to learn why she'd left him. He had hardly dared to imagine she would still want him, still love him.

Once they'd corrected their clothing, she sat in his lap on the grass, his cloak about them both. They sat like that, staring at the stars together, until the moon hung high in its ocean of sky.

She had finally told him. He'd waited six years to hear that explanation, and now that he knew what went wrong, he was determined not to lose her again. The fear on her face and the pain in her voice tortured him. He could see what years of living with such a secret had done to her, and it explained why the carefree lover of his youth was now so solemn.

As he twirled a lock of her golden hair around his finger, he realized that she'd told him everything about her situation, except for one thing—arguably the *most* important thing.

"How do you feel about it?" he whispered into the still night. "About not having children, I mean. Obviously, the lovemaking was incredible."

She snorted in laughter before looking up at him, her expression unreadable. "You know, you're the first person to ask me that."

Dallan's heart lurched. He rubbed her shoulders, waiting for her to think it over. After several moments, she tilted her head thoughtfully.

"I think a part of me keeps hoping I'm wrong," she replied at last. "Even though I know nothing can be done, I don't feel as though my heart's accepted it yet."

"What do you feel when you think about it?"

"Worthless, mostly," she admitted, her tone unflinching. "And I wonder what I did to merit such a fate."

"Your worth is not measured by how many children you have," Dallan replied gently. "Did you ever think that maybe you were meant to go through this terrible thing so that you could bring hope and healing to other women? Since I've come to Thurles, all I've seen is a strong, determined woman, doing her utmost to help everyone but herself."

She leaned back against him, her hand squeezing his. "I'd never thought it about it that way. Do you want children?"

"I honestly have never thought about whether I *want* them or not. I simply assumed it would happen on its own regardless," he said with a chuckle. "If I had a choice, though, I'm not sure. What about you?"

"I don't know. I've known for so long I wouldn't have them, that I've built a future in my mind without them."

Dallan wrapped both his arms about her, his face buried in her lavender-scented hair. "If you ever decide you want them, we could always foster. When I take the throne, it will even be expected."

He felt her tense in his arms. "Take the throne? I thought you were one of the Fianna now?"

"I won't be forever." He hesitated, doing his best to ease into the topic. He knew how she felt about it, how she'd always felt. When she'd left, he always assumed it had to do with his responsibility to Laigin, for she'd never shied from voicing her disinterest in becoming a queen. "Morda will expect me to return soon."

"And you intend to go?"

Dallan swallowed. "I want to marry you, Niamh. And I have a responsibility to my people, my family. I want you to come with me."

She pulled away from him, out of his lap, and turned to face him. "But, your family…" she began.

Dallan couldn't bear the stricken look on her face. After the first night they'd spent together, after they'd finally cleared the mistrust between them, he wasn't going to put anything else on her. He could speak with her in the morn, let her mull over the seed of the idea that he'd planted tonight. She didn't seem ready to hear about the details of his impending journey.

"It's nothing to worry over," he hurried, desperate to keep her worries away for just this one night. "Let's take another look around for that ghost flower, eh?"

She offered up a half-hearted smile, nodding in agreement. Dallan tried his best to push the conversation from his mind. She loved him. She'd said as much herself, proved it through her actions. He knew she'd come with him, even if she had her misgivings.

Beginning this night, Dallan vowed to help Niamh recapture the joy she'd once brought everywhere she went. He wasn't going to start by causing her more worry. When Dallan had struggled with his responsibilities as a young man, Niamh had always been there for him.

Now it was his turn.

CHAPTER TWENTY-SEVEN

THE FOLLOWING MORN, Niamh felt lighter than she had in years. She'd faced her deepest fear, told Dallan her darkest secret, and he'd loved her anyway. Standing before her work table, quietly grinding some dried nettles she'd collected on her outing with Dallan, Niamh thought perhaps her mother had been right all along. The faint woody scent of the nettles filled the chilly morning air, invigorating her and propelling her into the new day.

She always expected visitors to the infirmary. Long before the attack, folk wandered into her cottage for everything from cuts to coughs to labor pains. Though aches and ailments happened with frequency, Niamh strove to ensure they left as quickly as they came.

When Catrin entered the infirmary holding her head, Niamh wasn't surprised in the least that she already had a visitor so early in the morn, though she had yet to treat Catrin for anything.

"Good morning, princess," Niamh greeted her, setting down her pestle and walking over to the doorway. "Headache?"

Catrin nodded, wincing at the movement. "Worst I've had in ages."

"Have a seat over here, I'll make you something." Niamh gently guided her to a stool next to the work table. "You can lay your head down if it helps."

Catrin did just that, collapsing atop her arms onto the wooden table as Niamh set water to boil on the small hearth across the room. Once the water was started, Niamh dipped a cloth into a basin of cool water and wrang it out.

"This compress should help while you wait." She placed it where Catrin held her head, near her left temple.

Catrin thanked her before falling back onto her arms with a groan. Niamh didn't bother her as the water boiled and she steeped the herbs she had on hand—not her first choice, but hopefully enough to dull the ache. When the infusion was ready, she placed a hand on Catrin's arm to let her know and handed her a steaming cup.

"I'm afraid this is the best I can do for now," Niamh told her as she sipped the infusion. "Willow bark or a decoction would be better, but I haven't been able to gather those after my supply was destroyed."

Catrin's face fell. "I'm sorry."

Niamh smiled at her. "It's not as though it's your fault my cottage was ravaged."

Catrin swallowed a large gulp of her drink. Though she said nothing, the space between them filled with tension. Catrin's lips parted, as though she was about to speak, but she shut them and looked down at her cup instead.

Between her odd statement and even odder reaction, Niamh recalled the last time Catrin had behaved strangely. They had also spoken of the attack then, and Catrin had been at odds with her mother.

"Catrin?" Niamh settled onto the other stool at the table, folding her hands and focusing her attention on the young princess. "Is something the matter?"

"What if—" she hesitated, taking a breath, "what if it *is* my fault?"

Niamh frowned. "Catrin, Aodh's army destroyed the village at his command. It's no one's fault save his."

Catrin bit her lip, her eyes darting every which way. "It's *not* his fault," she replied, quiet yet emphatic. "And it's not all mine either."

Niamh fought to hide her shock at such a statement, knowing Catrin might stop talking if she overreacted. She was so close to getting the answers they needed.

"What happened?" Niamh pressed as Catrin sipped her drink. "Catrin, if you know something that we haven't been told, it's of the utmost importance that we hear the truth of it. I'd hate for more folk to die because someone hid the truth."

It was a stretch, she knew, putting such weight into whatever confession a young lady might have. Surely Catrin exaggerated, for Niamh couldn't imagine any scenario where the princess could possibly be the cause of the attack.

Catrin sniffled, her eyes reddening as tears threatened. She set down her cup, covering her face with her hands. "I can't take it anymore," she whispered, sniffling again. "She should have said something before the Fianna left!"

"Catrin," Niamh placed her hand on the girl's trembling shoulder, "I need you to tell me what happened. Start at the beginning."

NIAMH WOULD HAVE preferred to leave Catrin to quietly sip her curative while her headache subsided. Instead, she had no choice but to bring Catrin along with her to Dallan, who insisted she also attend the meeting he called in the solar. Niamh had no doubt that the poor girl's head ached from the strain of keeping such a secret. Hopefully, once they sorted this out she'd find some relief.

Well before midafternoon, the small solar at Thurles was packed, all the seats taken and a few folk standing. Catrin and Niamh sat while Dallan escorted Brona into the room. They had all met prior to decide how to handle the situation before summoning her to join. Cormac stood between the chairs and the blazing hearth, arms crossed over his chest. In spite of the seriousness of the meeting, Dallan winked at Niamh just as Cormac started to speak.

"Brona," Cormac began once the queen had taken her seat. "Some new information regarding the attack came to light recently, and I had hoped you or your daughter might be able to help me sort it out."

Niamh smiled encouragingly at Catrin, who looked as though she wanted to hide behind her chair. The girl's face was paler than the first snow of winter.

"Oh?" Brona replied, sounding utterly disinterested.

"You and your late husband invited Aodh to visit Thurles, did you not?"

The queen's eyebrows shot toward the ceiling, her lips twitching. "Wherever did you hear such a thing?"

"It matters not," Cormac replied tightly. "What matters more is your reason for inviting him. Is it true that you intended to hold him captive through trickery, luring him here under the guise of a potential betrothal before turning on him?"

Brona's face hardened. "I will not sit here and endure such spurious accusations."

"You deny it, then? That the attack on Thurles was in fact an act of self-defense by Aodh?"

"Of course I deny it!"

Niamh couldn't recall the last time she'd heard the queen raise her voice.

"We sent a messenger to Aodh, asking after the circumstances once we caught up to him," Cormac told her. "We asked your household staff for their accounting of events. We asked your fighting men who yet live. All told the same tale, that Aodh arrived peaceably days before the attack."

Though Niamh knew he hadn't done any of those things, she was grateful for Cormac's efforts to cover up Catrin's betrayal of her mother's secret. The young princess had been sobbing by the time she related her tale to him, and he had promised to do his best to conceal her part in all of it.

"I admit," Brona began cautiously, "that my husband and I had planned to capture Aodh and bring him to Brian as a gift. But Aodh had no knowledge of our intentions. He attacked without provocation."

"On the contrary," Cormac corrected her, "someone warned him the night prior, and from what I've heard your husband actually attempted to have him, an invited guest, taken prisoner."

Catrin had begun her tale to Niamh with that bit—that she'd felt so badly at her family's dishonorable betrayal that she had warned Aodh of their plans. Niamh could tell that Catrin's obvious infatuation with Aodh played a large part in her decision as well.

Cormac didn't wait for the queen to muster a response. "We must know the precise terms of the agreement you struck with him involving your daughter. Does he intend to marry her? Was it a betrothal?"

Though Niamh wasn't as well-versed in the matters of noble marriages as Dallan, she knew that such an alliance made without Brian's approval could wreak havoc on the kingdom. A match with Aodh, King of the Uí Neill, one of the nine kingdoms, needed Brian's involvement.

"Aye," Brona ground out. "But not to Aodh. He was taking her as a peace offering to Eochaid."

A collective gasp filled the solar.

"You traded her to Ulidia?" Cormac's voice wavered. "You know that man is a traitor, even to his own people."

"And what choice did I have?" Brona replied. "Die alongside my daughters, or exchange one and end the bloodshed?"

"The bloodshed *you* started," Dallan reminded her.

"He wouldn't have killed us," Catrin muttered, her eyes fierce. "He would have killed you, mayhap, but not Cara and me. You traded her for your own life and you know it."

"I gave her a choice!"

"I've heard enough," Cormac declared over the increasingly tense conversation. "Brona, you will be confined to your quarters until Brian arrives to dispense judgment. *You* are responsible for the deaths of your people and the endangerment of your daughter. Diarmid, Dallan, guard her door. I'll send word for Brian."

She watched Dallan's handsome face grimace as he walked out of the solar behind Brona. Niamh knew the feeling all too well. She, too, could hardly wait for Brian to arrive so that he would be off guard duty and back in her arms.

CHAPTER TWENTY-EIGHT

Dallan followed Diarmid and Brona up the nearby staircase to her quarters as his thoughts spiraled downwards. Morda expected him in Nás tomorrow, and he had planned to speak with Niamh well before leaving. He knew why Niamh had left, he knew what she feared, he knew what went wrong.

And, most importantly, he knew she still loved him. He hoped that was enough to convince her to go.

Since Morda visited him in Caiseal, requesting his return to Laigin and his oath as second, Dallan had been pulled in two. Like Eva, he cared deeply about their family back home. He had been raised with the understanding that one day he could rule of one of the nine kingdoms, that he would be responsible for the safety and welfare of his people. It was not a duty he took lightly.

Yet, Brian and his band of warriors now relied upon Dallan as well. He swore an oath of loyalty to join the Fianna, not imagining he'd be recalled to Laigin anytime soon. Eva, Finn, and all his closest friends needed him here.

It had seemed an impossible decision until Niamh reappeared in his life. Once he'd gotten past his anger at the pain she'd caused him, Dallan knew she held the answer he sought. If she would have him, he would stay—it was as simple as that. She had never wanted to be a queen, and now that he knew she worried over providing an heir, the decision was easier than ever.

Aye, he felt badly that he hadn't known before Morda exacted his oath. But he would explain everything to Niamh. Surely, she would understand.

Brona's terse farewell to them at her door snapped Dallan back to his current dilemma. He needed to speak with Niamh as soon as possible.

Dallan didn't have time to take a breath before Diarmid spoke.

"You weren't at the feast last night," his friend observed, looking at him pointedly.

"So?"

"Neither was Niamh."

Even worried as he was, Dallan couldn't suppress a grin at the thoughts that followed that statement. He could still hear the sounds she made, pressed against the cool stone, her breasts bouncing as he made love to her.

"Am I to assume matters have been…resolved?" Diarmid pressed when Dallan didn't answer immediately.

"Aye." Dallan's heart swelled as he remembered that she now wore his ring for good reason. "She finally agreed to marry me."

Diarmid's grin—the one notorious for charming even the most chaste ladies—lit up the dim corridor. He pulled Dallan into a quick but mighty embrace, smacking him hard on the back. "Congratulations, my friend."

"Warming up to marriage are you?" Dallan teased him.

"Yours, aye. I cannot be confined to one woman for the rest of my days, no matter how skillful she may be."

"When a woman finally does steal your heart, I'll take great joy in reminding you of what you just said."

Diarmid shook his head emphatically. "Impossible," he stated, as though falling in love were something he could control or predict.

"That's a bold challenge to fate, if you ask me."

"It's a simple fact," Diarmid replied. "I give my heart to every woman I take to bed. How could she steal something I already gave her?"

Dallan could only smile at his friend's ridiculous logic. The woman who tamed Diarmid would need to be a force of nature. If indeed he could be tamed at all.

"Do you think Brian will come tonight?" Dallan ventured.

As Diarmid was Cormac's brother, he may know something that Dallan did not. And anything Dallan learned could only help him right now. Aye, he was consumed with joy over his betrothal to Niamh—provided she still wanted to marry him after discovering his commitment to Morda. But he was also wracked with guilt over having to tell Brian that he had sworn to his uncle's service after spending so short a time as one of the Fianna. That Morda and Brian both knew that Dallan would have to break one of his vows didn't lessen the pain of delivering such news.

Dallan's hopes sank when Diarmid shook his head once. "No. He'll come first thing in the morn I'd wager. Can't wait to tell him, eh?"

If only that were the most important thing he needed to tell Brian. "Something like that."

They settled into a comfortable silence, Dallan bracing himself for a long night of waiting.

EVENING THREATENED BY the time Niamh left the solar, the sun's rays stretching toward the horizon yet not quite breaking it. How it had taken nearly a day to sort out Brona and Catrin's tales and get a full accounting, Niamh couldn't begin to fathom. She hadn't yet had time to tell Máire, Alva, or her mother about her magical night with Dallan.

Well, she likely would leave out quite a few details—like the bit where she cried out his name at the top of Cnoc Rua. Or how she'd been up so early because she hadn't slept at all. Or how right it had felt to be back in his arms.

As she neared the hall, Niamh decided perhaps it would be best to skip over the night and focus on the betrothal. Her mother, in particular, would be ecstatic. She'd always pushed Niamh to reconsider leaving Dallan, to give him a chance, to believe in him. To trust him.

She'd done all those things and then some. Only time would tell if she'd made the right decision.

Niamh opened the doors and stepped into the hall, her eyes adjusting slowly to the dim, fire-lit room. She didn't see her mother or Máire, but she spotted Alva sitting at the outermost table, far from all the other folk in the room. Her friend didn't appear to see her, staring blankly at her hands, her chestnut tresses out of their usual braids.

Niamh could tell instantly that something was terribly wrong. Alva rarely left her home, dedicated to helping her husband manage the smithy and always busy with housekeeping and her garden. When she had a spare moment, she used it to help her neighbors. Though her cottage had been destroyed, she'd continued her habit of near-constant activity, helping around the keep wherever needed. Niamh hadn't seen her sit down at all, aside from meal times.

"Alva?" Niamh ventured softly. "May I join you?"

Alva nodded, her face impassive.

Niamh sat beside her. "What happened?" she asked, keeping her voice low, so that no one could overhear them.

"She moved in." The pain in Alva's voice brought an ache to Niamh's chest.

"Oh, Alva." Niamh pulled her into the tightest hug she could manage. It seemed her good news would have to wait. Alva needed her support right now. "I'm so sorry."

"I didn't think he'd really do it," she muttered, her cheeks flushed. "Am I selfish, for wanting him to myself? A better wife would want what's best for him, want him to have children. That's why the law exists, is it not? To ensure the future."

"You are not selfish. Everyone deserves love and happiness.

Who is she? You've not said much about her, though I hardly blame you."

"The miller's eldest daughter, Úna."

"Well, perhaps when you conceive a child he'll see the error of his ways," Niamh offered, trying her best to comfort her friend in what seemed a hopeless turn of fate.

At that, a flash of silvery tears fell down Alva's pale cheeks. "I'm afraid that may be out of the question entirely now."

"What? Why? Alva don't say that. We can keep trying."

"I think I've the same problem as you," she leaned closer, her voice hushed. "My bleeding has stopped, too. It wasn't meant to be."

Niamh sat straight as a rod, excitement bubbling through her. "Alva," she worked to keep her voice calm, "if your bleeding has stopped, it's most likely because you are carrying, not barren."

"But I haven't felt ill at all," she countered. Though Niamh saw the light return to her eyes.

"Not everyone does. How long has it been since you last bled?"

"Not quite two turnings of the moon."

"Alva!" Niamh could hardly contain herself. "Why didn't you tell me sooner?"

"There was nothing to tell. Until this past sennight, it wasn't unusual. You know how unpredictable they've been."

"But this is the longest it's been between bleedings?"

Alva nodded, the dark look of defeat lifting from her face. "Do you really think it's possible?"

Niamh took her hands, feeling something she'd thought she'd never have again: hope.

"Anything is possible," she whispered, surprised to find that she meant it. "*Anything.*"

CHAPTER TWENTY-NINE

"LAY ON THE cot here," Niamh directed Alva. "I'll see if I can tell, though it may be too early yet."

Alva hurried to the cot, plopping down and chewing on her lip as she waited.

"Relax," Niamh instructed gently. "Just relax." She watched as Alva sank into a softer position on the cot, her hands unclenching as she took a deep, shaking breath.

"I'm trying."

"You're doing great." Niamh placed her hands on Alva's abdomen, putting light pressure on the area between her belly button and hips. She didn't expect to find anything. Typically the belly only started changing shape to the touch after three turnings of the moon. When she felt a slight swelling between Alva's hips, she squeaked in happy surprise, falling back to sit on her knees.

Alva's face glowed bright as she shot up. "What? What did you feel? Niamh, please, tell me."

"It's still *very* early," Niamh began carefully, "but I do think you're carrying. Is it possible you bled closer to three moons ago instead of two?"

Alva thought for a moment. "I suppose it could've been. I admit I haven't kept as good a count after you told me to cease my fretting."

Niamh beamed at her dear friend. "I'm glad you took my advice."

"So am I," Alva giggled. "It seems to have worked."

Though she knew she'd never be so lucky as Alva, she *knew* she could never conceive, something in the world felt right in that moment. More than any other woman she'd helped, Niamh felt a deep connection to Alva's plight. She had felt her pain as her own, her worry, her anguish. And now, she felt her joy as though she had fixed herself and not another.

"What do I do now?" Alva asked, her smile beautifully contagious. In all her years of mending people, she'd seen many happy faces. Yet none compared with those of a woman just told she would be a mother.

Niamh swallowed back the sting of knowing she'd never be one of them, focusing instead on Alva's hard-won victory.

"I have a whole list that we can go through, but you have only one thing to do the rest of the day. You need to go tell your fool of a husband that he no longer needs that other woman."

She watched Alva bound off to do just that, her chest swelling with hope for her friend. And joy for herself. She could hardly believe how well things had worked out with Dallan. She struggled to wrap her mind around the fact that she would be marrying him at last, with no secrets and no expectations. She'd taken the gamble, she'd told him everything, and she had won the love she'd always wanted.

Between all the day's meetings and her rush to check Alva, Niamh had missed both the noon meal and dinner. And she knew Dallan and Diarmid had as well. Instead of taking the small supper she'd normally have before retiring for the night, she went to the kitchen and begged three plates of leftovers from dinner. She could hardly manage the walk to Brona's chambers, where she knew the two warriors stood guard, between balancing the three platters and fighting the urge to fall face-first into the mouthwatering scents of honey bread and herbed salmon.

She had one more corner to turn in the corridor when she caught a snippet of their conversation. An alarming snippet.

"So Finn was right about Niamh?" she heard Diarmid ask, nearly causing her to drop the platters.

"Aye," Dallan replied, his tone clipped as though the topic brought him discomfort.

"He's always been good at concocting plans. At least now you know why she left. Still, I don't think I could've done it," Diarmid responded, "ignoring my anger like that."

"It was hard at first," Dallan's reply hit her like a punch in the gut. "But Finn was right. Kindness will always get you further than anger, no matter how deserved. And we always had a strong connection."

She should leave. She shouldn't have listened in the first place. Lord, she wished she could un-hear it. But her feet were frozen in place, her heart shattering as they continued.

"I have a strong connection with many women." Diarmid's tone made it perfectly clear what sort of connection he meant. "I highly recommend it. It certainly helps me avoid problems such as yours. Now you're stuck with one woman. *Forever.*"

Dallan laughed. *Laughed.* "It's not a problem. Not anymore."

She took several steps backward, somehow managing to keep hold of the platters as she turned and tiptoed back the way she'd come. What did he mean by that?

Was the problem her inability to have children? Was it that she'd kept it a secret? She thought they were finally past all that. Tears welled in the corners of her eyes as her mind raced to understand what she'd just overheard.

He'd assured her it didn't bother him, but maybe it was all part of this plan of Finn's that they'd mentioned. Was he only pretending to forgive her to learn her secret? Maybe he wasn't alright with it after all, and he'd only said he was because he'd been hiding how he really felt this entire time. Her father had done it expertly for years. She'd believed that he loved her and her mother right up until the day he left.

Now you're stuck with one woman. Diarmid's taunt usurped her thoughts.

It's not a problem. Dallan's easy reply.

Niamh swallowed the bile rising in her throat. Dallan had said he'd never leave her—though at this point she wasn't certain she ought to take him at his word—but he'd said nothing about not taking another wife. Did he plan to keep Niamh for fun and some other woman for heirs?

She didn't know what all this plan of Finn's entailed, other than playing her for the fool and planting more secrets at the foundation of their relationship, but it was clear that whatever he'd said, Dallan was not being forthright about his feelings.

A hole opened in the center of her chest, one that had been lurking in the shadows ever since Dallan came back into her life. Of course it was too good to be true.

One day. She'd had one day of bliss before her rash decisions came crashing down around her. In the end, just like with her father, she hadn't been enough.

Once she was well away from that part of the keep, Niamh broke into a run. She ran past her mother and Máire, whose heads whipped to follow her. She ran past Catrin, sitting morosely before the hearth in the feasting hall. She ran straight to the infirmary, finally empty of patients, crawled onto one of the pallets, and cried.

How could she have been so foolish? How could she have believed he could still love her, really love her, once he'd learned that she was broken?

By the time all her tears had come and gone, and she lay curled up on the pallet with Morrígan beside her, Niamh realized that her mother had been right. Dallan wasn't like her father. He was worse.

Instead of telling her to her face that she wasn't enough, he'd gone and told his friends.

CHAPTER THIRTY

SOMETIME NEARING MIDNIGHT, Cormac and one of the keep's guardsmen appeared to relieve Dallan and Diarmid from their posts. Between spending the night before with Niamh and staying up half this night on guard, Dallan barely made it to his bed before he collapsed. He woke shortly after dawn to the news that Brian had just arrived with his entourage and had called a meeting in the solar.

He found the king deep in discussion with Cormac. They stood in the center of the room, Cormac nearly a head taller than the grey-haired warrior king, whom Dallan had come to respect over the past months. He could hardly believe he was leaving Brian and the Fianna.

Walking over to join them near the small hearth, Dallan intended to beg a private word with Brian prior to the meeting, to tell him of all that had transpired. Instead, Diarmid, Catrin, and Brona filed into the room. It seemed his news would have to wait.

The disgraced queen sat in silence as they once more repeated Catrin's story and relayed to Brian the details of the meeting yesterday.

"Is that the truth of it?" Brian demanded of Brona when all had been told.

"All but the barbarian's crimes, aye. He still set Thurles ablaze, murdered innocent villagers, killed my husband."

"Men have started wars over smaller slights than that you

paid Aodh," Brian growled, as angry as Dallan had ever seen him. "We're lucky he only took one hostage. Do you realize how much danger you've placed this kingdom in? He was less than a day's march from Caiseal! You invited him without permission, you broke the sacred vows of hospitality, you began the battle that destroyed your holding, and you betrothed your daughter to one of my enemies without my involvement. A just man would have you pay with your life for such treachery."

The color slowly drained from Brona's face as Brian laid her crimes out plainly. And, to Dallan's thinking, the king had the right of it. The woman had endangered more than just her daughter with her scheming.

But Dallan knew that Brian, though just, was also tender-hearted. As much as he tried to hide it, the king ended feuds with marriages and hostages as often as possible to avoid unnecessary loss of life. He'd deny it with all the vigor left to him and he'd boast of all the foreigners he'd slaughtered, but he couldn't hide it from those who knew him best.

And, by some odd twist of fate, Dallan now counted himself among those close to the king.

"However," Brian continued, cutting the thick silence like a boat through still waters, "Your daughters have saved you."

"What?" Brona croaked, her hoarse voice filled with surprise. "How?"

"Catrin, at great personal risk, admitted to warning Aodh of your ill intent against him. She, at least, behaved as a host ought and enabled him to escape with his life."

Brona swallowed, eyes wide, as she frowned at Catrin. She pursed her lips, and Dallan decided she might be literally biting her tongue to keep from getting herself into more trouble.

"And then there's Cara, who sacrificed herself to save what remained of the family you destroyed," Brian continued. "I will not reward your daughters' honor and selflessness with your death. Instead, you will live out the rest of your days at the monastery of Cill Dara."

"Thank you," Brona managed, her tone icy.

Dallan waited with great curiosity for the end of Brian's speech. He and Diarmid had debated who might be made king of Thurles, but no one really knew what he intended. Dallan caught Diarmid's gaze as Brian started speaking again.

"Now, then," the king declared, "we arrive to the matter at hand. I am here to establish new leadership in Thurles. After giving it great thought. I believe we can create an opportunity from this misstep. Provided Cara yet lives and my Fianna can retrieve her, she will be queen of Thurles.

"I have threatened Sitric of Dyflin with a betrothal to strengthen our alliance for months. Cara will go to Dyflin to marry him, and he will gain Thurles among his assets. Finally, Catrin," the king turned to speak to her directly, "you will act as steward of Thurles whenever your sister is absent."

It was a brilliant solution, Dallan realized, though he knew Diarmid would be as shocked as he was by the appointment of the two princesses as queen and steward of Thurles. Dallan would wager Brian's previous marriage to his aunt, Gormla, may have something to do with his willingness to name a queen over a king. That Gormla had survived marriages to two of the nine kings of Ireland, and a possible affair with a third, and now helped her son Sitric rule Dyflin was a testament to the strength of women. She and Brian had both had too much fire in them to last, but Dallan knew the king still respected her.

Dallan hung back, standing near the door as everyone filed out. He shut it after Cormac left, making a mental note to find him and say farewell before he left for Laigin.

"It concerns me that you're frowning," Brian said, sitting in the nearest chair.

Dallan joined him, taking a seat in the chair opposite. "I don't want to leave."

"But you are." It wasn't a question.

"Aye. Fachtna, Baeth's father, is causing trouble," Dallan explained, though it only sounded like an excuse to his own ears.

"He's angling for my uncle's throne."

Brian leaned forward at the mention of Baeth. "That bastard who tried to kill me?"

"That's the one." During their final trial before taking their oaths as warriors of the Fianna, the men defended Brian from an attempt on his life by Dallan's own cousin. It had been too near a thing. Luckily, Finn had stepped in, or else the battle may have turned disastrous.

"I knew there was division over the throne," Brian said, "but I hadn't realized Baeth's father was the source of the dissent."

"If he takes it, make no mistake, he'll march on Mumhain within a sennight. Morda needs a second to strengthen his position. He has no one else."

Brian rubbed his chin, moving the bristles on his trimmed grey beard. "Have you already sworn to him as second?"

"I have."

The king's brow furrowed deeply. "Then I see no way around it," he admitted. "But you do realize you and Morda are both in danger until this is resolved, don't you?"

The small part of Dallan that had held out for a different resolution deflated in resignation. "I wish it were otherwise, but I cannot let the kingdom collapse into civil war, danger or not."

"No," Brian agreed, "you cannot. It would destroy more than just Laigin. If you can find some way to ensure Fachtna never takes the throne, you are always welcome among my Fianna."

They both stood, moving toward the door.

"I will do my best," he promised, though at the moment it felt futile.

Brian smiled sadly. "You always do. That's why Morda needs you."

As Dallan embraced him, Brian spoke under his breath. "A word of advice from an old king to a future one: Treat them all like your top man, but don't trust a single one."

Dallan thanked him and took his leave, finally beginning to understand how Brian had managed such a long and successful reign. If fate did intend for him to be a king, it would be a mighty feat to be half the king Brian was.

But there wasn't time for musing. He'd have the next day or two to strategize as he traveled to Nás, the royal seat of Laigin.

At present, however, Dallan faced the most difficult conversation of all, the one he'd been dreading for days.

He strode across the fog-shrouded courtyard, headed for the infirmary.

CHAPTER THIRTY-ONE

AT SOME POINT in the night, Niamh had slipped into a fitful sleep. She hadn't dared return to the room she shared with her mother and Máire. She wasn't anywhere near ready to face them yet, to be barraged by questions to which she didn't even know the answers. Though the notion of lying on the cot for the next few hours, wallowing in her heartache, felt awfully tempting, Niamh knew that wasn't the path to healing.

What had she told her mother when her father had left? What had she told Alva when her husband announced his plans to marry a second woman?

She'd told them those fool men didn't deserve them anyhow. Then she made them a warm, steamy infusion of mint leaves with lavender and roses. So, instead of curling up like Morrígan on the cool, rough floor, Niamh stood and put a pot to boil over the infirmary's small hearth, desperately missing the cozy little cottage that sat in a pile of ashes and broken dreams somewhere beyond the keep.

Niamh had just started gathering dried lavender and rose petals when Dallan walked in, his broad frame filling the doorway. She didn't look up from her table, dropping a pinch of lavender buds into her smooth stone mortar. She felt his presence behind her, watching her work over her shoulder.

"What's wrong?" he asked.

"Nothing," she lied. She still hadn't decided how to tell him what she'd overheard, though she began contemplating it, knowing the inevitability of the discussion this morn.

"There's something I should have told you," he began hesitantly, his voice pained. "I knew it would upset you, so I've put it off longer than I ought."

Niamh stilled. Perhaps she wouldn't be the one to bring it up after all. "Best get it over with, then."

Dallan blew out a heavy breath. "Brian and Morda each gave me a choice before I arrived in Thurles—join one and reject the other. Morda wanted me to swear the oath and become his second, Brian wanted to adopt me as his son so that I will remain with the Fianna and never rule Laigin."

Niamh's mouth fell open. How could it not? She'd expected a confession about whatever ploy he'd concocted with Finn, about how he concealed his true feelings about her infertility. Not this. Not more secrets. She could hardly believe it, though at this point she shouldn't be surprised.

"Niamh," he pleaded with quiet insistence, "will you look at me, please?"

She turned, still not ready to face him but accepting that she no longer had the choice. She did manage to close her mouth, at least.

He ran a hand along the back of his neck. "Two days ago, Morda returned to have my answer, and I discovered that the situation in Laigin is far worse than I'd realized."

This time her eyes did meet his, her voice flat. "You're leaving."

Of course, he was leaving. He'd gotten what he wanted, hadn't he? His answers, his closure.

"I swore to Morda, aye. He needs my help, or Laigin may go to war with Mumhain." He bit his lip—an act that would have undone her composure in any other scenario. "Before I knew that you returned my affection."

Before Samhain. Before he'd bedded her. He'd said he known two days ago.

"You knew you were leaving?" she asked in disbelief, her

voice rising in spite of her efforts at calm. "You knew on Samhain you were leaving?" Had he been planning this all along?

He stepped toward her, reaching for her.

She stepped away. "Why didn't you say something?"

"I tried," he replied. "I tried to tell you on Samhain, but I got so caught up in it, in you. By the time I had another chance, it was too late. It's no excuse, and I'm sorry."

"You could have told me before Samhain," she accused, blinking back tears.

"Could I, though?" he countered, keeping his voice slow and steady. Careful. "Niamh, you hardly spoke with me at first after I arrived. If I had told you, within days of you deciding to let me back into your life, what do you think would have happened?"

"So it's better to upset me after I've started trusting you? To lie to me to win my trust?"

"Of course not," he replied. "But you aren't the only one who had to decide to trust. Can't you see how afraid I was to lose you again?"

"So is that why you pretended that you liked me?" She was done with this, with him. Her voice shook in spite of her best efforts. "Was this all some sort of elaborate plot of revenge? Win her back, convince her to divulge her deepest secrets, bed her, then leave her as she did you?"

"What?" He looked genuinely confused, but Niamh knew better. "What are you talking about? Niamh, I really do love you."

"I heard you. Last night."

"Okay," he said, exaggerating the word. "What did you hear, exactly?"

He wasn't going to trick her again.

"I heard Diarmid ask about some plot you and Finn concocted to trick me into trusting you. And that being stuck with one woman—with me—was no longer going to pose a problem."

He ran a hand down his face. "That is *not* what Finn suggested. Diarmid was trying to be funny."

"Well, I wasn't amused," she shot back. "What *did* Finn suggest, then?"

"That instead of being miserable and angry while I was with you, I should see it as an opportunity for closure. He suggested that I *genuinely* be kind to you, explain that I wanted to know why you left, and hope that you would take pity on me. At no point was I trying to trick you."

"Then why does it still feel like a betrayal?"

Dallan's gaze softened. "Because, perhaps, you hoped all along that I wasn't angry with you, that a part of me still wanted you. Or, perhaps it isn't my forgiveness and acceptance that you need. Maybe it's your own. All you've been doing since I arrived in Thurles is look for reasons to keep pushing me away."

"Perhaps," she allowed. "But I'm having an awful lot of trouble unscrambling this mess. When were you only pretending to be nice? How long were you so angry that you would have avoided me instead of showing kindness? How much of what you said to me was even true? And," she declared, her mind and heart still reeling, "how does any of what you just told me excuse you keeping so many secrets from me when we were supposed to be starting over?"

"It doesn't," he answered without hesitation. "And I'm sorry."

"I told you everything." Niamh felt her composure slipping, her chest cracking open and summoning tears she'd never let him see.

"I know. And I want to discuss this more."

"But instead, you're leaving me."

"No." He whispered softly. "I'm asking you to come with me."

That stopped her retort, leaving her with her mouth hanging open. Again. "You thought that after you kept a secret like that from me that I would leave my family, my home, to live with a man I barely know?"

He stepped closer, and this time she held her ground. "You

know me better than almost anyone, Niamh, and I wouldn't have it any other way. I hoped that after you learned how much I love you, you might consider spending your life with me, even if it meant leaving."

A thousand responses raced through her mind, a thousand waves crashing against a rocky shore. But only one rose to the surface. "Goodbye, Dallan," she whispered.

For just a moment he looked so vulnerable, so sad, that she nearly tried to comfort him. But it was only a moment. His face hardened as he turned to leave.

"Goodbye, Niamh."

CHAPTER THIRTY-TWO

I T HAD BEEN almost a year since Dallan had last been to Nás, the seat of the king of Laigin. He'd ridden through the palisade with his father, on their way to aid Sitric in the battle in Dyflin against Brian. Predisposed to melancholy after that last conversation with Niamh, Dallan sank into that memory, one of the last he had of his father, who died in the battle less than a sennight later. His father's deep blue cloak had covered much of the horse as Dallan followed him into the bustling market town. He could almost see it in front of him now as he rode the same track.

Fate had an odd way of twisting back on itself. Now Dallan was a sworn warrior in Brian's elite guard, coming to help prevent a battle with him. Dallan's sister, who had never wanted to marry, had fallen in love with his best friend—whom he hadn't even known a year ago. And, perhaps craziest of all, he'd just lost the love of his life. Again. This time, however, he was the one who had to leave.

He wanted to spend a full fortnight drinking away her memory in the nearest tavern. He wanted to charge into battle, to run drills until he couldn't move his arms.

He wanted her back.

If Morda didn't need his support so badly, Dallan would fall into despair just as he had the last time they parted. He knew he should have told her. He understood her fear and anger. But, as he'd explained, trust went both ways. And until that night on the hill, Dallan didn't know if he could trust her with his heart again.

As it turned out, he couldn't. But it was a bit late for that realization.

Aside from its renown as a meeting place of kings, Nás had gained fame as a market town, connecting the shipping port at Dyflin to the center of the island. Clouds filled the sky, threatening rain across the rolling farmlands, as Dallan dismounted at the stables. It had been a hard day's ride from Thurles, but he didn't want to keep Morda waiting. He'd missed dinner, the sun already setting, but the light supper served before bed would be most welcome.

The sky finally opened as he entered the hall. His aunt Tuala kept a meticulous house, the rushes always fresh, the tables always clean, the fires always burning. The feasting hall at Nás was a large circle, just like all the halls built by their ancestors, with great wooden beams and trusses supporting a domed, thatched roof. Mismatched benches and chairs encircled the impressive central hearth and trestle tables filled the nearer half of the room.

His aunt and uncle sat before the hearth, surrounded by the lesser kings who answered to Morda. He recognized most of them, including Fachtna. His cousins, too, sat together playing a game of knucklebones at one of the empty trestle tables.

Bran, the eldest, looked like his mother with chestnut hair and eyes to match. Though tall and broad like most men in Dallan's family, Bran was no warrior. Neither was he a scholar. Indeed Bran's brother, nearly half his age and rather a surprise to his parents, appeared to be winning the game.

Carvill, just shy of sixteen, had all the makings of a future king but none of the experience. Untried in battle, still deep in his studies, and still growing into his own skin, he'd make a fine king after Dallan. But he was not prepared for the storm about to break, which is why Morda had called in Dallan.

Fachtna spotted Dallan first, standing up straighter, like a bird spreading its feathers. His posturing was so ridiculous Dallan would have laughed if he didn't pose a real threat to Morda's reign. Recalling Brian's advice, he swallowed his annoyance and nodded a greeting to Fachtna. The shock on his face was worth the effort.

"Dallan!" His Aunt Tuala called, rising from her seat near the fire to embrace him. "Oh, I could hardly believe it when Morda told me you were coming back. We're so glad to have you."

"Aye, we are," Morda agreed with a smile to match the fire's warmth. "Come, you've had a long journey. Let's see what the kitchens have left."

The moment they were out of earshot of the hall, Morda turned to Dallan as they walked. "How did it go? You look tired."

"Brian couldn't have taken it better," he said, keeping his voice low. He'd seen servants milling about and didn't know how many could be trusted.

"I noticed you came alone," Morda replied, more hesitant than usual. "I'm sorry. Truly, I am. We needn't speak of it. Women can be more dangerous than a battle."

Dallan couldn't agree more. "A battle I'm finished fighting," he grumbled.

"We'll talk more of women and the meeting once you've rested. The council is still arriving, and we can spend tomorrow plotting while they get settled. The meeting will be the following morning. Hopefully, it will give us enough time to consider our options," Morda told him, opening the door to the kitchens. "Now, then. Let's see what Miryam has for us."

Dallan didn't have even a moment to process his uncle's flood of information before Miryam, the cook of Nás for as long as Dallan could remember, greeted them warmly. She pushed two plates full of honey cakes, apples, and oat bread across the table where she worked. "I was just putting together everyone's supper. Shall I have yours sent to the solar?"

"No need," Dallan told her with a wink, grabbing the plates. "I think I can manage it."

"You're carrying mine," Morda declared, holding the door for him. "The last thing I need is for the lot of them to see me trip and fall while carrying my own supper."

As they made their way to the solar, where they were guaranteed the privacy needed to begin discussing the particulars of Fachtna's dissent, Dallan finally had a moment to close out the miserable day. Aye, it was wonderful to spend time with his family. He had always enjoyed Morda and Tuala growing up, and though he didn't know Carvill as well as Bran, he had always had a close bond with his cousins.

And he knew how badly Morda needed his help. In a way, he was aiding Brian as well by coming home to prevent an overthrow of the men sworn to him and a descent into war. But even surrounded by kin in his childhood home, even knowing how important his presence was here, it did not soften the loss of those closest to him that he'd left in Mumhain.

He was well and truly separated from Eva and Finn, the Fianna, Brian, and the life he'd started building. He thought he'd fight beside the Fianna for years, maybe a decade or more if he were lucky, taking the throne when Morda passed. Unless he were summoned to Mumhain or Finn and Eva requested special leave, he would never play with his first niece or nephew. He'd no longer see the sister he loved so dearly that he'd been willing to give up everything to save her. He'd never fight beside Finn again.

He'd never see Niamh again.

Looking at the plates he carried, his stomach turned sour, his appetite gone. He felt now the full force of his carelessness. Even knowing what had gone wrong the first time, he'd managed to lose her again. Maybe she was never meant to be his after all.

CHAPTER THIRTY-THREE

ONCE BRONA AND Catrin told the true story of the attack, life in Thurles changed overnight. The same day that Dallan left, Cormac lifted the ban on travel outside the safety of the keep before he and Diarmid headed north to aid the Fianna in their rescue mission. It felt as though Niamh breathed in and life was filled with Dallan and the Fianna, her days spent in the keep. She exhaled and it was all gone, all different.

Brian decided to remain in Thurles until Cara returned. Niamh's respect for the king only grew as she watched him spend hours teaching Catrin proper stewardship of the castle. The princess knew much of what needed doing to run the keep, but she hadn't been instructed in politics or warfare. It would be a difficult transition, no doubt, but Niamh believed in Catrin's ability to hold the keep. And, more importantly, so did Brian.

Niamh should've been happy that life had finally returned to normal. She, her mother and Máire could rebuild their cottage. Niamh could see patients from the comfort of home, surrounded by her herbs and tinctures. She could continue helping women live healthy and happy lives.

Instead, she wandered the wreckage of the cottage beside her mother and Máire, feeling a kinship to the destruction around her. Like the village, she, too, would need to rebuild. But not today.

Today she was still burning.

"Niamh?" Máire called softly, lifting up something so small

that Niamh couldn't make it out. "Come look what I've found! You'll never guess what it is."

Niamh reached down to scratch Morrígan's chin as Máire bounded over a pile of logs, cupping something small in her hands. She opened them like a blooming flower, revealing one entire stick of cinnamon.

Tears welled in the corners of her eyes.

"No, Niamh," Máire soothed hurriedly. "Oh, don't cry. I'm sorry." She wrapped her arms around Niamh, rubbing her back. "I thought you'd be happy to finally find it."

Her mother set down the cloth she'd been inspecting and came over, hugging Niamh from behind.

Niamh let the tears fall, shaking inside their warm arms, encircled by people who loved her. "Why didn't he tell me?" she cried, her voice whisper-thin and entirely too fragile. "Why did he have to leave?"

She knew the answers, of course. But knowing and feeling were two entirely different matters. And right now, she could only feel. Loss. Betrayal. Hurt. Anger. Confusion. So many thoughts whipped back and forth within her, but none made it any easier to accept that he was gone.

That he had left her.

Niamh supposed, in a darkly ironic sort of way, he'd finally gotten revenge—now she knew *exactly* how it felt.

"Do you want to talk about it?" Her mother asked.

"Not really," Niamh sniffled, stepping away from them and wiping her eyes with her sleeves. "Let's just get cleaning. I want to forget about it."

It had only been a few days since the battle, hadn't it? How could her world turn upside down and then back again in such a short time?

She knelt to help clear the rubble, sorting the pieces of their life into piles around them.

It had been the same way when she first met Dallan—her life had transformed overnight. Their connection had been equally intense and immediate, as though from the moment she met him she couldn't remember her life without him.

Sensing her melancholy, Morrígan rubbed her little grey body against Niamh's legs, squinting up at her through gorgeous green eyes. She gave the wee thing another good scratch behind her ears, ignoring memories of Dallan gifting her the kitten in a box under the trestle table.

"Maybe you should take a break, dear," her mother suggested, wiping her own brow.

"I'm fine," Niamh replied. "Really," she added when her mother looked at her like the liar she was. She was absolutely *not* fine, but that wasn't going to keep her from pulling her own weight.

Her mother relented. "I've made a pile of the herbs I could find, and some of the jars and baskets and such. Why don't you have a look through it?"

Niamh followed her mother's gesturing to find baskets and broken jars filled with a jumble of stems, leaves, and flowers. She wouldn't be able to salvage all of it, but it was certainly a start.

"Where did you find them?" she asked, walking over to get started. "I looked through here twice already."

"Most of the herbs over by your worktable were burned to ash," her mother replied. "I found these under the wall that collapsed. The mud must have protected them, or the fire had burned out in time to spare them."

They worked for several hours, spending much of the morning and part of the afternoon salvaging, sorting, and stacking until they could once again see the earthen floor.

"A good day's work," Máire declared as they stood in a row, each one's arms behind the other, looking at the results of their efforts.

"A good day, indeed," her mother agreed. "Shall we head to dinner?"

"I'm going to go find Alva," Niamh replied. "I'll meet you in the hall."

She'd been so wrapped up in her own problems that Niamh had nearly forgotten about Alva.

Wandering down the dirt path to Alva's cottage, Niamh found her doing much the same as they had, sorting and piling debris. Niamh's stomach dropped when she noticed that Alva was joined by her husband—and another woman. The look on Alva's face as she raised her head, eyes meeting Niamh's across the way, said it all.

Apparently, her husband was more of a fool than Niamh had believed. Or more selfish, at least.

Plastering the biggest smile on her face she could manage, given the circumstances, Niamh swooped in for the rescue.

"How are you feeling? Have you eaten enough, taken some rest?" she asked Alva a little too loudly. "You don't want to overexert yourself."

Alva sighed, setting down an armload of broken wood on the nearby stack, and meeting Niamh in the road. "It's no use," she muttered under her breath. "But I appreciate the effort."

"If you told him, why is she here?" Niamh narrowed her eyes at the pair of them.

"He's ensuring his succession," Alva replied, clearly mocking his own answer to the very same question.

Niamh scowled. "He's a blacksmith for god's sake!"

"The king of the forge," Alva grumbled, her lips thin.

"The fool of the forge, more like." Niamh put her arm through Alva's, turning to call back to the pair of them. "I'm stealing her!"

Alva's husband frowned at Niamh's joke, making her feel just a tad bit better. Even the corners of Alva's lips lifted.

"I'm not angry with him," Alva admitted as they walked arm-in-arm toward the keep. "Just sad and a little powerless. Naught can be done, and he's acting entirely within the law. He's been as kind about it as possible, but..."

"But he isn't above breaking your heart so that he has a son to pass his trade to," Niamh finished for her.

"Precisely." Alva paused, furrowing her brow. "I heard that the Fianna went north."

Niamh's chest constricted uncomfortably. "Cormac and Diarmid went north. Dallan went east."

Her mouth opened in shock. "To Laigin?"

Niamh nodded. "He left yesterday."

"Oh, I'm so sorry! Why didn't you say anything?"

"I didn't want to dampen your joy," Niamh snorted. "Though it seems your husband's done it for me."

"He left without you?" Alva sounded angrier over Dallan leaving than her husband taking another wife. "What did he say?"

"Well," Niamh blew out a breath, "he asked me to go with him."

"And you *didn't?*"

"He kept it from me!" Niamh defended. "*And* I discovered— entirely by accident, mind you—that he'd only been nice to me after the battle to try to learn why I'd left him. I'm also not entirely sure he meant what he said about not caring that I couldn't have children, as he was lying to me the entire time. That he knew he was going to be leaving days ago and he never told me was just the half of it. I suppose it's fair though, since I did the same when I left him."

Alva nodded, her face pinched like she didn't quite agree. "Is it, though?"

"Is it what?" Niamh could already sense she wouldn't like where this was headed.

"I'm going to give you my opinion, and you're not going to like it, but I think you need to hear it."

Niamh swallowed, preparing herself. "Go on."

"It's not the same at all," Alva said gently, her voice kind though her words hurt. "When you left, you didn't tell him why or give him the choice of following. When he left, he explained his reasons and asked you to come with him."

"Perhaps," she allowed, "there is some truth in what you say." More than some. Too much. Niamh's head spun as she thought through Alva's observation. "But what of his feigned friendship?"

"Can you really blame him?" Alva questioned, her tone still soft. "He had no reason to believe you wanted anything to do with him. And if, as you told me, he's never stopped caring for you, then seeking closure to his pain is not unreasonable. *And*," she added emphatically, "kindness is certainly better than anger."

Niamh did not like how much sense that made, not at all. Because, if Alva was right, then she had made a grave mistake.

"Do you love him?" Alva interrupted her pondering.

She was angry and hurt, aye, but Niamh knew she'd never stop loving Dallan. She nodded slowly.

"I am powerless. I cannot change my foolish husband's mind. I cannot do aught but live my life the best I can with another woman in the house. *You* are not powerless here, Niamh," she declared, her voice growing in volume alongside her conviction. "You can create the life you want. You can still go with him."

Niamh's head felt too light, like it would float away. "Go to Laigin? But I don't want to be a queen," she said, horrified. "They'll be *expecting* an heir! What if I went and they don't let us marry? Or what if he's changed his mind now that he knows he'll take the throne?"

Alva stopped walking, placing both her hands on Niamh's shoulders. "He knew already," she reminded Niamh. "You said yourself he knew days ago that he'd be leaving. Which means he knew he would be king when he told you he loved you, when he spoke of marriage. He won't change his mind, and something tells me his family won't be able to do a thing about it."

She wanted desperately to believe Alva, fighting to keep her fears at bay. "Do you really think so?" she whispered, her mind not yet grasping what her heart had all but decided.

"Niamh, I would hate to see you go, but I wouldn't have suggested it unless I knew it was the best thing for you. You have taken care of me and countless others for years. You've helped me heal, helped me conceive, helped me cope. Let me return the favor. Let me help you."

A tentative smile broke across Niamh's face, spreading as slowly as the idea Alva had planted. "Máire and mother will be upset."

"They'll manage," Alva assured her, smiling for the first time that day. "It seems we have some packing to do."

"Aye," Niamh squeezed her friend's hand, "it seems that we do."

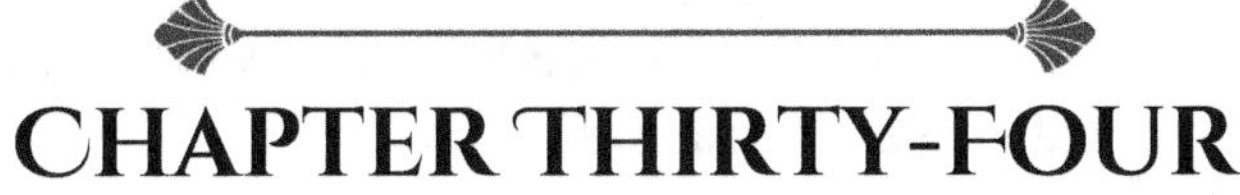

CHAPTER THIRTY-FOUR

ORDA WAITED FOR Dallan outside the feasting hall, the courtyard eerily silent in the early morning. Fog hung heavy over the keep, a dense chill in the air. The hall had been emptied for the meeting, all the lesser kings of Laigin summoned. The small council, as they were known collectively, weighed in on the king's decisions. Many spent weeks at a time in Nás, offering counsel as needed. Others visited only when summoned.

This grey autumn morn, Morda called them to hear the news of Dallan's appointment as second. After discussing the situation at length over the past day, Dallan knew they stood at a disadvantage.

As Fachtna even now vied for the throne with an alarming amount of support, he would be favored as the choice for second. A fact that he would no doubt point out. But Morda couldn't risk naming him as second. It would create the perfect opportunity for Morda to meet an untimely end, with Fachtna assured of his accession to the kingship.

"Ready?" Morda asked, opening the door without waiting for Dallan's response.

In sharp contrast to the somber courtyard, the hall was a shock of warmth, light, and life. The central hearth blazed as usual, as did braziers at intervals about the room. The tables were arranged so that the longest sat in the center, between the hearth and the door. Nearby, another table was laden with roast boar, apple tarts, and honey mead. The members of the council, fifteen in all, milled about in idle conversation.

The soft murmur of voices subsided as Dallan entered the room behind Morda.

"Thank you all for coming on such short notice," Morda began. "I'm certain you remember my nephew, Dallan. I've called this council to inform you that he has sworn the oath as my second and will take the kingship after me."

Dallan watched their reactions closely. All were telling.

The kings whose settlements fell nearest to Nás and Dyflin, where Dallan had spent much of his life until this past year, took the news in stride. One or two even smiled. Dallan knew them the best, and had seen them often growing up, but they made up the minority of the council.

Everyone else reacted poorly. They crossed their arms or frowned. An alarming number of them looked to Fachtna for his reaction.

And he did not disappoint.

"You named the second without consulting the council?" he asked, his shock striking Dallan as more performance than anything else.

"Aye," Morda replied evenly. "I am the king, after all. The council advises. I decide."

Fachtna took several steps forward, crossing his arms. "Yet you did not seek our advice."

"The decision was a simple one. I didn't require it."

"Still, we should have been consulted." This time it was Donnchad, king of the Uí Kinsella, who spoke up, earning a nod of approval from Fachtna. The Uí Kinsella were a rival branch of Dallan's kin who had lost the throne three hundred years ago and were desperate to regain it. Apparently, they hoped to do so by siding with Fachtna.

Several other men voiced their agreement with Donnchad's statement.

"I'm sorry, brother," Morda said. "Dallan was the right choice."

"You know my claim is stronger," Fachtna shot back.

"By law your claims are equal, and you seek only to divide instead of unite."

"If we had a common enemy to unite against, it would be a simpler task," Fachtna spat. "But you've seen fit to get in bed with that enemy."

Dallan had heard enough. Stepping forward, he took up Morda's defense. "You would rather be at war? Throwing men's lives away instead of working toward prosperity and peace?"

Fachtna's sharp gaze pierced Dallan. "And where have you been this past year? You disappeared after the battle, and last I saw you, you raised your sword *against* your kinsmen."

"Only the oath breakers," Dallan replied.

He and Morda had feared this turn in the discussion, as Fachtna's son, Baeth, had died in that battle only a month earlier. Baeth led a contingent of warriors from Laigin, whom Brian had asked to join him as allies. Instead, Baeth's men turned on Brian and nearly killed the king.

"Sitric mentioned that you fought with Brian, not Laigin." Fachtna's lips curled upwards. "As one of his Fianna."

Everyone, even those who had been in favor of him as second, broke into a chaos of concern over that statement. Dallan hadn't been in contact with any of his family once he'd learned that his sister was Brian's captive. He'd set out to rescue her, by any means, in the end joining Brian's group of elite Fianna warriors. It wasn't a decision he regretted, nor did it necessarily disqualify him from the kingship.

Not normally, at least. But the look on Fachtna's face told Dallan that nothing about this discussion would proceed 'normally.'

"Don't grieve for your son by punishing your nephew," Morda warned.

"Does it not concern you that he is sworn to Brian? To a man making every effort to steal the high kingship and rule all Éire?"

"You and I have also sworn to Brian, Fachtna. As well as all the rest of you," Morda reminded the council. "Following the battle, we all swore oaths as allies."

"The oath of an ally," Donnchad began, stepping forward beside Fachtna, "is not the same as the oath of a Fianna. Dallan has sworn to defend the king's life, to carry out missions in his name, to further Brian's plots, perhaps even against our own men. If he is so dedicated to another kingdom, how can he rule his own?"

"Indeed," Fachnta agreed, "how could he be expected to ride to battle against Mumhain if the alliance should fall? He would be little better than Brian's puppet. We may as well call ourselves men of Mumhain, for Laigin would be consumed by Brian's beastly ambitions."

A roar of agreement and anger followed that ridiculous speech as a cold sweat overtook Dallan. The bastard was actually winning over the council. Though Morda had the final say as king, going against the council could put him in danger. According to ancient laws, a king could not rule if he were not of sound body, leading to many cases of blinding, or worse, stealing the throne from an unpopular ruler.

The men of Laigin had taken the loss at Dyflin hard. And now they were placing the blame soundly at Morda's feet. He understood their mistrust of his position—Dallan had gone and sworn fealty to the man who'd crushed them in battle and forced an alliance. Even to Dallan it sounded outrageous.

That was when he realized that he and Morda could not win this debate. Aye, they could bring in a brehon, a master of the laws, to judge the case, and likely he'd rule in favor of Morda and Dallan. But that wasn't the true cause of the dissent. Fachtna wanted Morda off the throne, and he was using Dallan to get it. Even if Dallan stayed on as second, he feared for Morda's safety.

"What is it you want?" Dallan asked, tired of his incessant arguing. "You've voiced many complaints yet offered no solutions."

"To my mind, you've committed treason twice over," Fachtna declared. "First, when you swore your sword to Brian without the council's approval, and again when you took the oath as second knowing of this conflict of your loyalty."

The rush sounding in Dallan's ears distracted him from Morda's livid response. He saw the king's face growing redder as he argued on Dallan's behalf. They had both predicted the council turning on Morda.

Neither had foreseen the men turning on Dallan.

He watched the arguing between them grow more and more heated, knowing he had no choice, really. The punishment for treason was death.

It was his life or Morda's. It was his life, or war for his people—in two kingdoms. If Morda agreed with Fachtna and sentenced Dallan, he would at least gain the council's respect once more.

Dallan stepped forward, raising his hand to signal for silence. "I willingly accept the judgment of treason and its consequences," Dallan announced, hardly believing he'd just uttered those words. "And you will witness the respect your king has for you in his acceptance of your will and cease undermining him, lest you, also, become oath breakers."

The rest of the meeting passed in a blur as they decided on his method of execution for the morn. Morda caught him alone once everyone had dispersed, more distraught than Dallan had ever seen him.

"What are you thinking?" he demanded. "We could have found another way! Surely, we could have convinced them."

Dallan wished it were so, but he knew there was no other way. "I won't be the reason you lose your life or your kingdom."

"And I won't be the reason my favorite nephew dies tomorrow. Come, Fachtna has agreed to a private meeting."

Several minutes later, Dallan, Morda, and Fachtna sat in the solar at Nás, glaring at one another.

"I know what you want," Fachtna taunted.

"A resolution wherein our nephew doesn't die?" Morda

growled. "Aye, and it's what you should want as well. He's your family, and you and I both know you're only going after him in an attempt to weaken me."

Fachtna sat back, his face hard as he turned to Dallan. "I'm sorry you've been caught in the midst of this, boy, but it's what needs doing. Morda, you know I should be your second. Kinship always passes between brothers before generations. It may not be law, but it's tradition."

"If I made you my second, you'd murder me and crown yourself before marching our people to slaughter at the hands of Mumhain," Morda replied, his voice unnervingly calm.

"I could kill you right now and take the throne," Fachtna retorted, "but I would likely lose much of the support I've worked for from the council. The same is true if I were to kill you as your second."

Dallan didn't like that they'd somehow passed over the issue of his execution and were now speaking solely of murdering one another. He cleared his throat, interrupting Morda. "What can we do to convince you to stay the execution?"

Fachtna shook his head. "The council has spoken, and I do believe you've overstepped your oaths. If Morda goes back on the sentence now, he'll only seem weaker. And, as you observed, many of the councilors already see how weak he has grown since Dyflin."

Morda's face reddened, his lips thinning. Dallan imagined the king was even now contemplating Fachtna's death over such a bold statement.

"Peace and weakness are not one and the same," Morda ground out. "A peaceable man, who does not draw his sword at every slight, is far stronger than one who gives into such base behavior."

"Alright, peaceable man," Fachtna sneered. "Name me as second, swear to declare war on Brian at the first opportunity, banish this oath breaker from Laigin, and make arrangements to retire to Armagh. Then, perhaps I will see if I can sway the council from execution."

Dallan scoffed aloud. "Ironic, don't you think, that you call me oath breaker when you plot to break your oath of truce to Brian?"

"Spoken like his hound," Fachtna spat.

"That's an insult, not an answer," Dallan said.

Dallan could see Morda's frustration as he watched his kingdom slip from his hands. A year ago, before the defeat at Dyflin, Morda could have simply overturned Fachtna's demands and the council would have supported him in doing so. But now, they were as likely to turn on him and seize the kingdom for themselves as to stand behind him, perhaps more so. He couldn't risk it, or he'd be risking war.

"Here are my terms," Fachtna began. "If Dallan is executed, and Morda allows the council to choose his second, I swear Morda will come to no harm."

"Unacceptable," Morda snarled, his patience clearly waning.

"Here are *our* terms," Dallan declared, casting a quick glance at Morda before staring down Fachtna. "If I am executed, you will cease vying for the throne and undermining Morda's rule. You will never become his second, and no harm will come to him. The council will choose his second, so long as it is not you. They will be made aware of this bargain, and if it is broken they are within rights to punish you with your own execution. You will get to make a spectacle of me, as you clearly desire. You will get to win this ridiculous power struggle by doing so. And you will not have Brian's hound within your kingdom, advising your king."

Morda's face fell, his eyes grim. Fachtna looked from his brother to Dallan before nodding.

"Agreed."

CHAPTER THIRTY-FIVE

S HE WAS LOSING her mind. Absolutely, undoubtedly, going crazy. Even as she rode into the courtyard at Nás, Niamh couldn't believe she'd done such a thing. Thanks to Brian's intense campaigning over the past decade, travel within the kingdom was relatively safe, even for a woman on her own.

Máire and her mother had made Niamh promise to send for them if everything went well on her arrival, and they would come join her in Nás. Until then, they would remain in Thurles and salvage what they could from the wreckage of their cottage.

Swallowing her doubts, she dismounted, handing her horse to the groom and wandering toward the building he'd told her was the hall.

This was her chance, she reminded herself. She could stay instead of walking away again. She could choose Dallan, a future with the man she'd always loved. This time, she wasn't running away.

Pushing open the doors, she found the hall more crowded than she'd expected. A number of men, most older and well-dressed, milled about the cavernous room. The undulating murmur of conversation had a lilt to it that told Niamh something was happening in Nás, something worthy of more gossip than usual. Spotting a group of servants in the process of clearing a table of platters of food and pitchers of ale, she decided to investigate.

"Excuse me," she approached a young woman carrying a

platter of roast boar, "I'm looking for Dallan mac Murrough. Do you know where I could find him?"

The woman's eyes went wide, her face stricken. "You'll need to speak with his uncle, the king. Morda is in his solar. This way."

The woman led Niamh into a corridor at the back of the hall, opposite from the courtyard entrance. They passed two doors, stopping in front of the door at the corridor's end.

"What's your name, miss?"

Niamh answered her, watching as the woman knocked and then entered, announcing Niamh and then ushering her inside. The door shut quietly behind Niamh as she stood facing a hearth in another, smaller, round room. A man of an age with Brian stood in the center of the room, his face drawn and weary. She recognized him as Morda, though he had aged noticeably in the six years since she'd left Nás.

"Welcome, dear Niamh," he said with a sad smile. "It's been far too long since I last saw you."

He gestured for her to sit beside the crackling hearth, and she quickly complied, uncertain what to expect from this odd meeting. She'd expected Dallan would be relatively easy to find. She'd never imagined she needed to go through the king to see him. Though, she supposed, it made sense, especially if Dallan had told his uncle about her inability to produce heirs. If Morda was determined to prevent their marriage, this was his best chance.

Folding her hands in her lap, she steeled herself for a battle. She wouldn't be swayed so easily, and she wouldn't leave without seeing Dallan.

"What brings you to Nás?" he asked, not unkindly.

"Dallan invited me, before he left," she explained. "I thought it over and realized that coming here with him was the right decision."

Morda sat down across from her, leaning forward intently. "In that case, I'm afraid I've terrible news."

Niamh swallowed. It was just as she'd expected—a battle. But this time, she was ready to fight it.

"The small council met this morning," he told her. "I summoned them to tell them of Dallan's appointment as my second. They did not take the news well."

Niamh sat up at that. "What do you mean?" Perhaps Dallan had been released from his obligations. Mayhap even now he was on his way back to Thurles.

"The man who wishes my throne went after Dallan, rallying all the kings behind him," Morda explained, his voice cracking. "Dallan is to be executed for treason in the morn."

"What!" Niamh shot out of her chair, utterly incapable of accepting something so sudden. And so ridiculous. "He's done nothing wrong!"

"As Dallan and I both pointed out to them. But they are out for blood, and it was mine or his. I tried to intervene, but you know Dallan."

Of course, she did. He would never let anything happen to those he loved. He would never think twice about stepping in to shield them from harm, even at the risk of his own life. He may have left Brian's service, but he was still a Fianna at heart.

"Can you not call a brehon?" Niamh's mind raced, her heart hammering so loudly she could hear it in the room, could feel it across her whole body. "What of a fair trial?"

Morda went through the entire meeting in great detail, explaining to Niamh the precarious political situation in which they found themselves. And for which Dallan had sacrificed himself in an attempt to save Morda and preserve the peace.

"So, what you are telling me," Niamh said, fighting to keep her voice steady, "is that unless I can devise some method of rescue, Dallan will be killed at dawn?"

Morda nodded, his head hanging. "If you've any idea of a way out, I beg you to share it. I would do anything to reverse this wretched sentence."

Niamh forced herself to breathe slowly. Panicking wouldn't save Dallan. This was what she did, wasn't it? She helped people.

It felt so surreal, so unexpected, that the full force of it hadn't quite hit her yet.

"It's a struggle for power between you and Fachtna, aye?" she asked, an idea beginning to form in her mind.

"Aye," he agreed. "One that Dallan's been caught in the midst of."

"So, it's based on your reputations?" she pressed, growing more excited. "Your sway with the other council members?"

"What are you getting at, dear?"

"It may not work," she admitted, "but I do have an idea. What if I were to find a way to make Fachtna instantly and irrevocably less desirable as a leader? Do you think that would be enough to get Dallan released?"

He rubbed his chin, sitting back in his chair and narrowing his eyes. "There's no way to know how such a ploy would be received. I used to think the council wise, but it concerns me how quickly Fachtna has won them over. They resent Brian's hegemony, and Dallan symbolized that when they discovered he was oath-sworn to the man who'd killed their sons in the battle at Dyflin."

The small bubble of hope she'd managed to conjure popped. Niamh looked down at her hands, willing an idea to her. She had always been the instigator, the plotter. She had always been the one spurring Dallan onward to adventure.

Morda tilted his head, regarding her with a kind look. "However," he continued, "I have a plan to win back their goodwill, regardless of Dallan's fate. If we can save him, and if you can somehow lessen Fachtna's sway, then I can manage from there."

His words sparked a thought. Which led to another. And another. Within moments, Niamh had finally devised a plan, though she knew it was one that Dallan would never willingly follow, no matter how much she goaded him. Hopefully, Morda would be more accommodating.

"I have an idea," she told him, "but it's quite risky."

"Dangerous or uncertain?"

"Both," she admitted.

"Then let me take the risk," Morda offered. "Dallan would kill me himself if I let harm come to you."

Niamh pulled her lips tight. "It has to be me, or it won't work."

"Then at least tell me what you're thinking, so I can devise a way to support your efforts."

"Only if you swear not to try to stop me."

"On my honor," Morda replied, leaning forward intently. "Now, tell me what you've got in mind."

CHAPTER THIRTY-SIX

IN SPITE OF giving her his word, Morda did attempt to talk Niamh out of her plan, though he admitted it held promise. She was grateful that he discussed the details with her, for his knowledge of the people and politics involved gave her some confidence that, even if it went poorly, Dallan could still be freed by her efforts.

By the time they'd finished meeting, it was long past dark and Niamh's stomach growled as she stood to leave the cozy solar. Morda walked her to the kitchen, piled her arms with as much food as she could carry, and led her to the room where Dallan waited.

Thinking this was his last night.

Niamh's heart lurched at the idea of him feeling so desolate, of being faced with such an unthinkable burden. She wished she could tell him of their plan, give him some small hope that perhaps things would change.

But she and Morda had agreed that Dallan couldn't know the plan, for he would almost certainly intervene. And, though it may temporarily lift his spirits, success was not guaranteed. So, though she couldn't share her plan to free him from his sentence, she could share the night with him. No one should be alone on what they believed to be their last night.

They reached his door and Morda told the guards that Niamh was allowed to come and go as she pleased. Thanking him, she stepped into a small chamber, lit by a brazier in one corner. Furs covered a generous bed on a wooden frame, so large it took up much of the modest room. A stool and a small, empty table had been squeezed into the slim space between the bed and the wall.

More impressive than the soft furs, however, was the man lying atop them. Dallan reclined on the bed, his hands behind his head, his mess of dark waves catching the flickering light. When he saw Niamh, a heart-melting smile spread across his face.

He rose from the bed, hurrying over to take some of the food from Niamh's arms and set it down on the table. His arms were around her before she could thank him, squeezing her so hard she laughed. Picking her up, he carried her to the bed and they tumbled onto it.

"How are you here?" he asked, kissing her instead of waiting for her reply.

Niamh sank into the bed beneath him, savoring the feel of his lips on hers—soft and demanding. She ran her hands through his tousled curls, something she did at every opportunity.

He pulled back for just a moment, cupping her cheek in his hand.

"I realized that even though you left Thurles, I was the one running away," Niamh told him. "And I'm not going to run anymore."

His head dropped to her chest and he let out a shuddering breath. "I fear it may not matter."

She lifted his face up again, brushing back his wild hair with her fingers. "I spoke with Morda already." She hesitated. It pained her to see him this way. "He's working on a plan to stay the execution, but it's not for certain. He's doing everything he can."

"That sounds like him," he replied, mustering a smile that didn't reach his eyes. "He's not putting himself in danger, is he?"

"No," she assured him, which was entirely truthful. "But I propose we make a rule for the rest of the night."

He snorted. "No speaking of tomorrow?"

"Precisely," she said. "No matter what happens, I say we make this night spectacular."

"What did you have in mind?" he teased.

"Dinner, of course," she replied in kind, moving as though she intended to go grab the basket of food she'd brought.

His hands found her sides, tickling her until she laughed so hard, she could barely breathe. Once she finally did catch her breath, he captured it, his mouth moving over hers once again.

This time, she knew it was more than just a kiss. Something in his energy shifted, his muscles tightening beneath her fingers. How had she ever thought she could live without him? She needed him like she needed air, and she had been suffocating slowly for years without even realizing it.

Her hands slid beneath his *léine*, allowing her to feel his hard body. With a wicked grin, he helped her take the garment off. Niamh took a moment to simply stare in amazement. She couldn't fathom the hours he must spend in the training yard to look like that, but she certainly appreciated it. It kept him alive.

And made her breath catch every time she saw him naked.

"That's not fair at all," he whispered, his kisses trailing down her neck.

Niamh slipped off the bed, dropping her clothes to the ground with a wiggle. The chill air in the room had her hurrying back to his waiting arms.

Dallan's responding groan sent tingles down to her core. He pulled her back to the bed, his trews somehow disappearing in the process. Assaulting her senses, it felt as though he were everywhere at once. His hands brushed her breasts, followed by his mouth. Niamh's body responded to his touch, her mind incapable of thought. The feeling of his desire pressed against her belly left her feeling hot and empty all at the same time.

When he finally entered her, the fire building in Niamh grew unbearable. As they moved together, she savored every moment, every sensation, every sound, every movement, tucking the memory away and praying she'd never need it.

"I love you," he whispered, his voice deliciously rough.

Niamh tried to reply, but that proved her undoing. Instead,

the world seemed to stop, fading to darkness before bursting with light. Before the room stopped spinning, she heard Dallan moan, thrusting himself to the hilt.

"I love you, too," she finally managed as the room came back into focus. They laid like that, frozen in time. Niamh wouldn't speak of tomorrow, but as she looked in Dallan's eyes she saw the same despair she felt.

What if her plan failed? What if she couldn't save him?

Dallan's hand rose to her cheek again, his chestnut eyes softening. She could see her reflection in them, like staring into pools in the deepest part of the forest. He swallowed, opening his mouth to speak, but Niamh put her hand on his lips.

"Let's get some dinner," she said, forcing her voice to sound far cheerier than she felt. "I'm starving."

CHAPTER THIRTY-SEVEN

DALLAN WOKE FEELING as though a boulder had settled in the pit of his stomach. He didn't want to be second. He'd never wanted to leave Thurles. He wanted to wake up every morning next to Niamh, spend his days fighting alongside the Fianna to help secure Éire from further invasions, and hold Niamh in his arms every night. But if this is what he must do for his family, then he would do it without complaint or remorse.

He had held her tight against his chest the entire night, lying awake through much of it and soaking in her closeness and warmth. He'd gone over the situation a thousand times in his mind, until he'd finally succumbed to exhaustion, yet he still hadn't devised a solution.

Perhaps Niamh was right, and Morda had some devious trick lying in wait. But yesterday after the council meeting his uncle seemed defeated, not determined. And though their meeting with Fachtna had done nothing to alter the rule of the council, it had at least secured Morda's hold on the throne. It was best not to let his hopes run away with him.

He brushed a lock of her golden hair off her face, tucking it behind her ear and planting a soft kiss on her head. How lucky he'd been to have such a rare woman love him not once, but twice, in one lifetime. If only he could keep her.

Looking out of the small window, Dallan saw soft light playing at the edge of the horizon. Perhaps if he thought of this moment at the end, it would be where he spent eternity. It was certainly worth a try.

Summoning his courage and doing his damndest not to think about anything but Niamh, Dallan quietly slipped from the bed and dressed. He debated whether or not to wake her, but a loud rap on the door made the decision for him. She shot up, pulling the wolfskin blanket over her bare chest.

Dallan strode over to her, kissing her so thoroughly she'd remember it until they met again.

The door opened, interrupting the kiss. Morda and Fachtna walked in with four guards. Dallan appreciated that not one of them commented on Niamh's presence or her state of undress.

"Time to go," Fachtna said, reaching for Dallan's arm.

Dallan threw off his hand. "I'm able to walk myself," he growled.

Morda's face was drawn but unreadable as he turned to Niamh. "We'll be at the edge of the town, near the forest."

"I'll be there," she replied, glaring at Fachtna.

On a different morning, Dallan would have had a laugh over the look she gave that bastard, as though she planned to murder him in his sleep. And mayhap she did, for all Dallan knew. He'd learned years ago never to underestimate Niamh.

Entirely too soon, he'd said his goodbyes to her one last time before walking out of the town to the forest's edge. A crowd had already gathered there, and more followed behind them. Dallan's heart rose to his throat when he spotted Niamh hurrying down from the village, her blue woolen dress whipping about her the whole way, golden hair the same color as the rising sun. He'd told her she looked best in blue.

The crowd formed a circle about Dallan, Morda, and Fachtna. It seemed all of Nás had turned out to see the spectacle. Taking several deep breaths to steady himself, Dallan searched for Niamh in the crowd that had seemingly swallowed her whole. He heard the sound of a sword being drawn behind him, and Morda stepped forward to address the crowd.

Before he spoke a word, Niamh stumbled through the front

line of onlookers, her face as pale as new milk, her lips tight.

"I wish to address his accuser," she shouted, taking one step closer to Morda. The crowd went silent, all eyes on her.

Dallan's blood ran cold. He didn't know what she planned, but he knew Niamh well enough to guess that it wasn't anything he'd wish her to do. She'd said his uncle had a plan—was this a part of it? Perhaps they'd conspired to help him. Morda was wise and cunning. A great man, a great king. But Niamh was downright devious. Out of practice, certainly, but Dallan had seen the schemes she'd come up with over the year they'd spent together in Nás.

Fachtna stepped forward beside Morda. Dallan wanted nothing more than to punch that smug look off his face. "What can I do for you, dear?" he asked Niamh, testing the strength of Dallan's willpower.

"You can fight me," she declared. "I challenge you to a duel for Dallan's freedom—from his oath and his execution."

Well, that answered that. "Absolutely not," Dallan interrupted, looking to the guards to ask them to take her up to the keep before she got herself killed alongside him.

Morda raised a hand. "It is Fachtna's decision to accept the duel or risk destroying his reputation."

"Are you attempting to goad me into slaughtering an innocent woman?" Fachtna asked incredulously.

"Are you using my sex to hide your cowardice?" Niamh taunted him.

Fachtna looked from Morda to Niamh, his mouth agape. "Can you even lift a sword?" Fachtna asked.

Niamh drew a small sword, little larger than a dagger, from a sheath Dallan hadn't noticed about her waist. God's bones, she was really going to do it. He couldn't just stand by and let her throw herself on Fachtna's sword for him.

He moved to interfere, only to find himself held on either side by a pair of guards. He looked to Morda, who shook his head subtly. What game was he playing?

If Fachtna refused a duel, he would be a coward and lose the respect of his followers. If he killed her, he'd be the man who slaughtered an innocent woman. If he lost, Dallan would go free. Of the three, losing was his best choice, but Dallan wouldn't underestimate the man's thirst for blood. It seemed Morda and Niamh were betting on his pride over his bloodlust.

Devious, indeed.

Dallan's breath faltered as he watched Fachtna draw his sword and advance toward Niamh.

NIAMH WAS A damned fool. Her heart hammered against her chest as she sucked in a shaky breath and adjusted her grip on the small sword Morda had given her. The crowd behind her roared as he accepted her challenge, raising his blade and advancing across the small circle.

Out of the corner of her eye, she saw Dallan glaring at her in shock, his mouth a tight line. She couldn't think about that, or she'd lose her nerve. Better she die fighting for his life than live her own without him. It was a decision she made the moment Morda told her about the execution. It had been, aside from loving Dallan, the easiest decision she'd ever made. And almost certainly the most foolish.

Morda assured her that the odds were low that Fachtna would kill her outright. Aye, he might injure her, but he'd lose the respect of his mob of followers if he slaughtered a woman fighting for the man she loved. Which was why it had to be Niamh. If Dallan or Morda had challenged him, it wouldn't have trapped him between his reputation and Dallan's life. Only Niamh could buy Dallan his freedom.

They met in the center of the circle of onlookers, who cheered wildly as Fachtna circled her, a wolf stalking a lamb. He lunged at her, his sword flicking in her direction. Slowly.

Deliberately.

She blocked him with a haphazard swing of her sword.

He repeated the attack on her other side and she again blocked him. He was toying with her and everyone knew it. She might not know a thing about swordplay, but she refused to appear the coward. Niamh charged him, her sword pointed at his heart, a shout escaping her as she ran.

He easily knocked her sword aside, smacking her bottom with his own as she tumbled past him, losing her balance. The crowd laughed. Dallan started fighting with his guards, trying to pull his arms free, but two more joined the others to keep him in place.

Niamh stood, charging Fachtna again, this time aiming low. Once again, he deflected her attack. This time, however, he let his sword catch her arm, drawing blood. She cried out, grabbing her arm, and the crowd began yelling.

They liked the entertainment, but it seemed they didn't want to watch her lose. Fachtna read them as well as she expected of a politician, holding a hand to calm their cries and dropping his sword to the ground. He raised his fists, motioning Niamh to come at him.

She dropped her own sword, as she was useless with it anyway, and ran at him again, the crowd roaring to life around them. He landed a hit on her chest, knocking her onto her back and stealing the breath from her. Bringing to mind a memory she'd not soon forget. Oh, aye, she had thought back many a time to when she'd seen Dallan in the same position, seven years ago in the training yard on the day they'd met. As quickly as she could, she spun her legs into Fachtna's.

Knocking him onto *his* back.

And just like that day in the training yard, the crowd roared to life about them. He lay there, shocked, listening to the crowd cheer her on. Niamh knew he could rise and beat her to death without any trouble. But they both knew if he did that, he'd lose all the support he had for the kingship.

So instead he raised his hand, leveling her with a murderous look. "I yield!" he shouted, doing his best to make a show of it for the crowd. He stood, waving to the men and women who clapped and whistled. But even as he smiled for them, he leaned close enough that only Niamh could hear his words.

"You've saved your man, I'll grant you that," he whispered, "but now his uncle is left unguarded."

"Luckily Morda is cleverer than you," she shot back. "And so am I." She left before he could respond, already wondering how in the world she could dishonor him enough to keep Morda safe. Niamh didn't take two steps before Dallan had scooped her up in his arms, kissing her until the crowd was good and riled, leaving her breathless.

"You," he breathed into her ear as he set her down, his voice rough, "are in so much trouble."

CHAPTER THIRTY-EIGHT

DALLAN KEPT HIS hands firmly about Niamh's waist, hardly able to believe it was finally over as the crowd rushed toward them. His heart, his mind, his very soul felt ravaged by the whirlwind of the past few days. He held her to him as they stood, a rock in the sea of villagers.

"Dallan," she whispered, pulling his head down nearer her lips. "Your uncle."

Like a smith's hammer on steel, the realization of their actions struck him. If he had not been executed, then the deal had been broken. And Morda was once again in danger. More so, since Fachtna had been demeaned by Niamh's duel.

Spinning to find Morda in the burgeoning chaos, Dallan exhaled in relief when he spotted the king just behind his guards. Until he saw Fachtna behind the king. He dropped his hand from Niamh's slender waist, running to Morda's side.

Dallan watched Fachtna pick up his sword from underfoot, turning toward Morda. But he had not trained as a Fianna for the past year only to watch his uncle murdered before his eyes. He leapt through the crowd like a salmon upstream, forging a path, thinking of nothing but getting between Morda and that blade.

He was faster. He was stronger. He was better.

With practiced hands, he unsheathed a sword from one of the guard's belts as he flew past, bringing it down atop Fachtna's with chilling resonance. Morda spun around, his guards taking the wide-eyed Fachtna in hand as they realized what had happened.

"Shall I kill him?" Dallan asked, relishing the thought of ridding Morda of this nuisance once and for all.

Fachtna said nothing, his face ashen, his eyes murderous. Morda tilted his head, hands clasped behind his back, as he considered his brother.

"No," he declared at last. "The council resented the last time I left them out of a decision. This time, we will consult the people that Fachtna has worked so diligently to befriend." Morda turned, motioning for the guards to bring Fachtna before him and calling the crowd to silence. The space of one man was all that separated the kings from the people on the grassy field at the forest's edge.

"Fachtna has just committed treason, attempting to stab your king in the back," Morda began. His booming voice held everyone's attention. "The punishment for treason is death, as he reminded me yesterday. But he is family, and I would be willing to exile him instead of taking his life. Furthermore, though he refused to consult a judge yesterday, I wish to do so in order to uphold the laws of our people. Brocc, would you step forward?"

A tawny-haired man, small of stature, walked out from the crowd, inclining his head to Morda.

"What is the penalty by law for attempting to murder a man?"

Brocc stood straight, leveling a glare at Fachtna. "It is different when that man is also a king," he explained in a voice far louder than Dallan had expected. "For attempting to murder a man, with a weapon and before a crowd but without harming him, the fine is one pound of silver."

Several folks gasped, but Niamh looked to Dallan, and he could see she thought the same thing he did: it was far too small a price to deter Fachtna. Aye, it was more than the price of cinnamon, but Fachtna held lands in his own right. Such a fine would hardly register on his ledgers.

"For attempting to murder a king, should a hanging not be demanded, the fine is two pounds of silver," Brocc continued. "And, as an advisor of law, I would suggest that should he be fined instead of executed, he also lose at least one hand—the one that attempted to kill you."

"Ah," Morda nodded, a slight smile teasing the corners of his mouth. "A compromise."

A brilliant one, Dallan realized, impressed at the judge's cunning. To be a king, a man must be whole of body, according to the ancient laws. If Fachtna lost a hand, he would lose his own lands *and* he would no longer have a claim to the throne.

Morda turned back to the crowd. "You've heard the judge's advice. So now I ask you: Should we hang Fachtna? Or should we uphold the laws and the peace by demanding his hand and a fine?"

Shouts rang up to take his hand, drowning out nearly everything else, until it became a chant. Morda turned to Fachtna. "You heard them. It seems your people do love you after all." The king nodded to one of his guards, who pushed Fachtna to his knees in the center of the crowd, pinning his arm to the ground. Dallan saw Niamh cover her eyes as the guard's sword came down.

"OUR HEALER SAYS it was a good, clean cut," Morda relayed as Dallan and Niamh joined him in his solar later that afternoon. "And he's not gone feverish."

"Good," Niamh replied, frowning slightly. "If you want to keep him alive, though, the wound will need minding for the next sennight at least."

Dallan took her hand, offering her a small smile. He knew she was thinking of Tadhg and his leg.

"I met with the small council following the spectacle, and they requested that he also be exiled from Laigin."

That surprised Dallan. And also concerned him. Their support wavered too quickly, making them unreliable unless they were finally prepared to stand strong behind Morda. "Will you do it?" he asked.

Morda nodded. "I will, for it is a small request in the bigger picture, and it will win some of their goodwill back. They delivered the sentence themselves, giving him until he heals to remain in Nás. But," he added, sitting up straighter, his face brightening, "we have more important matters to discuss."

"You spoke to the council regarding the naming of your second?" Dallan ventured. He knew his position as second needed to be resolved, but he couldn't begin to guess how the council would feel about it after all that had happened.

"They saw the value in having a man with your skill set and training as second," Morda explained, "but they are still disapproving of your connection to Brian."

"What would you have me do? What would help you most?"

"You've helped me plenty," Morda told him. "The council has agreed to uphold my decision in making you my second, should you desire it. If not, they expressed interest in appointing Carvill. The choice is yours, with my gratitude."

"Will Bran feel slighted?" Niamh asked, not familiar with either of Dallan's cousins. "Is he not the elder?"

"Oh, heavens, no!" Morda chuckled. "Bran would sooner join a monastery than become a king, though I doubt he'd enjoy either. No, he'll support his brother, likely grateful the burden doesn't fall to him."

Dallan knew in his heart what he wanted, and he didn't hesitate when Morda turned to him for his answer. "I want to go home," he replied, "and as much as I love my family and my people, Laigin is no longer my home. In fact, I wish to formally renounce my claim to the throne."

"What?" Niamh asked quietly. "Dallan, are you certain?"

He looked at her, his golden-haired healer. "I'm certain. I know you worry over heirs. You've no desire to be queen. And all I want is to be with you." Dallan turned to Morda once more. "If you have need of me as a warrior, so long as it is not against Brian, I will come."

Morda stood to embrace him. "I'll make a nuisance of myself in Caiseal so I can visit often," he promised with a grin. "I need to check up on Eva as well."

"We would love that," Dallan said, returning his uncle's smile.

"You should come for the wedding," Niamh suggested, standing.

"I'm sure your aunt and cousins will wish it as well. They're sour over missing Eva's nuptials."

Dallan chuckled. "I told her to wait, but you know Eva."

"Aye. Once her mind is set, that's all there is," Morda agreed. "You send for me, and we'll be there."

THAT NIGHT, MORDA hosted a great feast—a betrothal feast, he declared it—to honor Dallan and Niamh. The hall at Nás was filled with light and laughter, singing and stories, and best of all, dancing. But Dallan knew it wasn't only their betrothal he was celebrating. He'd finally ended the strife that had run rampant in Laigin since the battle at Dyflin, and he'd done so without killing his brother or watching his nephew's execution.

Dallan and Niamh sat in the same seats as the first day they'd met, and it felt like just as much of a new beginning as it had then. Niamh settled beside him, still wearing the blue dress he loved. How could he not, when it reminded him so clearly of what treasures lay beneath it?

"I have something for you," he whispered, unable to keep from grinning.

He could tell that she sensed mischief right away. "Dallan," she warned.

Before she could continue her protest, he slid a basket to her beneath the table.

"You did not!"

"I did," he admitted. "I couldn't resist."

She opened the lid to reveal a small, mewling kitten, its orange fur the same hue as the firelight before them. Reaching in, she brought the wee thing to snuggle in her lap.

"Consider it both an apology, for giving you cause to doubt

me, and a thank-you for saving my life."

She squealed out something that Dallan thought might have been thanks as she lifted the kitten to her chest. "You name this one," she cooed.

Dallan shook his head at the sight of it. She was absolutely coddling that kitten, and Dallan enjoyed every second of it—and the bright smile it brought to her face. "We should name him, Aodh, obviously."

Her smile disappeared. "You jest."

Now it was his turn to laugh. "Not at all. That kitten looks like a lick of flame."

"But what of the Aodh we encountered most recently? You know, the one who burned my village to the ground?"

"I could have done without the village burning," Dallan replied with his wickedest grin. "But I owe him gratitude for one thing, and it's a big one."

"What, exactly, is that?" Niamh asked.

"He brought me back to you."

CHAPTER THIRTY-NINE

A SENNIGHT LATER, Niamh laid out a thick woolen blanket beneath an oak tree, wishing she'd brought just one more. It was a clear, crisp autumn evening, but the sun had taken all warmth with it when it sank below the horizon.

Dallan finished putting out their small campfire, built into the ground instead of above it to keep the smoke and flames from view. Then he strode up behind her and pulled her into an enormous hug.

"You look cold," he whispered. "Would you like me to warm you up?"

Niamh choked back a laugh, not wanting to make too much noise. "How often do you plan to use that line?"

Picking her up in his arms and laying them both down on the rough woolen blanket, he grinned at her in the filtered moonlight. "Every night we're out here, that's for damn sure."

"What if it stops working?" Niamh teased.

"It won't."

A breaking branch in the underbrush nearby brought the conversation to a sudden halt. Dallan grabbed his sword, motioning for her to stay put. She did, but she grabbed the dagger he'd given her. Just in case.

He crept in the direction of the sound, so silently she strained to see him as he disappeared around a thicket. Then she heard someone shout, the clash of swords, and a shocking amount of swearing before Dallan reappeared, two men behind him.

"Niamh!" Diarmid called under his breath, keeping his voice low and his tone congenial. "Nice to see you again."

"How'd you find us?" Dallan demanded.

Niamh nearly chuckled at the look of disappointment on his face at having been tracked by anyone.

"It's likely my fault," she offered.

"Nope," Diarmid replied, smacking Dallan's shoulder. "We spotted you from that hill this morning, so we backtracked." He gestured vaguely northeast.

"I suggested we find you and travel the rest of the way together," Cormac explained. "He suggested we give you a good scare first."

Dallan swore at Diarmid again, who grinned at him. It was too dark to see the details of his face, but Niamh knew his eyes would be sparkling with mischief. It was easy to see how he and Dallan had become friends.

"Sorry to interrupt you right before the fun," Diarmid said, "but I heard that line and it was definitely not going to work."

As Dallan and Diarmid dissolved into something between a wrestling match and a fistfight, Cormac walked over to sit beside Niamh. She and Dallan had been traveling for the better part of the last sennight, first from Nás to Thurles where they told Brian of all that happened. He happily accepted Dallan back, adopting him as promised, and giving his blessing on their betrothal.

They'd spent the next two days feeding and watering their tired horses and catching up with friends and family—among other things. Máire and her mother were happy to see her, but in truth they made a good deal more fuss over the kitten. Niamh knew little Aodh would be in good hands until she and Dallan returned.

Alva spent an entire evening filling Niamh in on what had happened in the few short days she'd been gone. Apparently, she'd discovered that her husband's new wife hadn't wanted the marriage either. In Alva's efforts to make the best of a bad situation, she'd grown close enough to the woman for her to confide in Alva—that she was in love with a man in the next village. When Niamh left Thurles, Alva and the woman were just beginning to hatch a plan to help her get out of Alva's house and married to her lover. Niamh thought she might tell the tale to Finn, without anyone's names, of course. Dallan had told her that he was a truly skilled bard, and it seemed like the sort of story that could fuel a ballad.

Cormac interrupted her musings, his voice quiet and kind. "How do you feel about undertaking such a journey?" he asked.

After they'd sorted things in Thurles, Brian had sent Niamh and Dallan north, to meet up with the rest of the Fianna. Brian expressed concern over the princess's health and general well-being once she was rescued, uncertain what to expect. He also thought she would appreciate a lady's maid while traveling in the company of so many men. As Niamh was a capable healer and always up for an adventure, she seemed the natural choice. The first day had been great fun as they rode through the northern part of Brian's kingdom and crossed back through Laigin. But this afternoon they'd entered the territory belonging to Brian's rival, King Malachy of Midhe and High King of Éire.

"A bit nervous," she admitted, watching with amusement as Dallan and Diarmid collapsed on the ground, their bout apparently over. "I'd feel better if I could defend myself, but I suppose that's what Dallan's here to do."

"We'll travel the rest of the way together," Cormac reassured her.

"I thought you'd have caught up with the others by now," she said, realizing how many days it had been since Cormac and Diarmid left Thurles.

"We had to make a detour," he explained. "And we spent today circling back for you once we spotted you."

"Well, we appreciate the company."

"Speak for yourself," Dallan grumbled, joining them on the blanket and pulling Niamh into his lap.

Niamh rested her head against Dallan's strong chest, listening to the casual banter between the three friends. She could feel his words resonate inside him against her ear, reminding her of the seashells that collected along the shoreline carrying the sound of the water wherever they went. The warmth of his arms surrounded her as she fell asleep, somewhere in Midhe on a chilly autumn night.

Out with Dallan, on their way to their next adventure.

About the Author

Sophia has been telling stories since she could talk. She loves learning almost as much as she loves writing, pursuing both her undergraduate and master's degrees. She has studied archaeology, anthropology, and the languages and histories of a variety of cultures. Her master's degree is in medieval history, with a focus on the British Isles. She's been fortunate enough to participate in three archaeological excavations and surveys–one at a Native American settlement in southern Indiana, one at a Tudor estate in Essex, and one at an early medieval ringfort in County Roscommon, Ireland.

After marrying her high school sweetheart, attending grad school, and moving nearly ten times in as many years, Sophia and her husband settled into a lake house in northern Indiana. When she isn't working on her next novel, you can find her in the garden and covered in dirt. They live happily in the middle of nowhere with two little boys, two atrociously rude doggos, and one ornery cat.

Facebook:
facebook.com/SophiaNyeWrites

Instagram:
instagram.com/sophianyewrites

TikTok:
tiktok.com/@sophianyewrites

BookBub:
bookbub.com/authors/sophia-nye

Goodreads:
goodreads.com/author/show/20815931.Sophia_Nye

Amazon Author Page:
amazon.com/Sophia-Nye/e/B08L9XZ148

Website:
sophianyewrites.com

9 781963 585179